Sum

'If I was in rea
'you'd help me c

'Sure,' I said, jerking my head back as her nose almost jabbed me in the eye.

She let out a relieved breath. 'Then you'll back me up, huh?'

'I guess so,' I said uncertainly. 'Back you up with what?'

'I don't have time to tell you right now,' she said. 'All you need to remember is that your name is Laine and that we live in Beverly Hills.'

'*What*?'

'And we've got an older sister called Stacy. And she's going to be starring in her own TV series, OK? Called *Stacy, Stacy*.'

I gasped. 'Amanda, what the heck have you been *telling* people?'

Little Sister books published by Red Fox

Book 1: The Great Sister War
Book 2: My Sister, My Slave
Book 3: Stacy the Matchmaker
Book 4: Copycat
Book 5: Sneaking Out
Book 6: Sister Switch
Book 7: Full House
Book 8: Bad Boy
Book 9: The New Stacy
Book 10: Summer Camp

Summer Camp

Allan Frewin Jones

Series created by
Ben M. Baglio

RED FOX

With special thanks to the following students of Pimlico School, who acted as story editors:
Gabriel Adesina, Mohammed Ahad, Verity Allison, Emily Bland, Jamila Bouchiba, Jack Catling, Jonathan Davies, Daniel Gleadall, David Holtam, Martha Singh Jennings, Susan Lovelock, Bria Muller, Shelby Roberts, Iyana Rose, Chantal Stević, Nicola Wells.

A Red Fox Book

Published by Random House Children's Books
20 Vauxhall Bridge Road, London SW1V 2SA

A division of Random House UK Ltd
London Melbourne Sydney Auckland
Johannesburg and agencies throughout the world

Copyright © 1996 Ben M. Baglio and Allan Frewin Jones
Created by Ben M. Baglio, London W6 0HE

1 3 5 7 9 10 8 6 4 2

First published in Great Britain by Red Fox 1996

This book is sold subject to the condition that it shall not, by way of trade or otherwise, be lent, resold, hired out, or otherwise circulated without the publisher's prior consent in any form of binding or cover other than that in which it is published and without a similar condition including this condition being imposed on the subsequent purchaser.

The right of Allan Frewin Jones to be identified as the author of this work has been asserted by him in accordance with the Copyright, Designs and Patents Act, 1988.

Phototypeset in Plantin by Intype London Limited
Printed and bound in Great Britain by
Cox & Wyman Ltd, Reading, Berkshire

Papers used by Random House UK Ltd are natural, recyclable products made from wood grown in sustainable forests. The manufacturing processes conform to the environmental regulations of the country of origin.

RANDOM HOUSE UK Limited Reg. No. 954009

ISBN 0 09 968871 9

Chapter One

I, Stacy Allen, of Four Corners, Indiana, would like to start by saying that I'd always wanted to go to summer camp. I'd wanted to from as far back as I can remember. And I'm eleven, so that's pretty far back.

I'd seen brochures and movies that made summer camp look like the greatest thing in the world. And friends at school would come back from camp with stories about how fabulous it all was. And I'd never been! Ever!

I'd also like to point out here, for the record, that my sister, Amanda, had always wanted to go to summer camp, too. And she's thirteen.

So, between us, my sister and I had spent twenty-four years wanting to go to summer camp. Oh, except for when we were babies like my baby brother Sam, and we didn't know what a summer camp was.

Last year we couldn't go because Sam had just been born and money was really tight.

The year before that we couldn't afford it because the local office where my dad worked had just been closed down and he was waiting to hear whether he was going to be taken on in the Chicago office or lose his job. (He got the Chicago job, by the way. He sells books to bookstores.)

I can't remember why we couldn't go in any of the years before that. All I know is that we *wanted* to and, for one reason or another, we didn't.

But this year, at last, both Amanda and I were going to summer camp! In fact, we were going to *two* summer camps. One each. Amanda was going to Camp Powhatan and I was going to Camp Yellowhammer.

'Yellowhammer's a weird kind of name,' Amanda's dumb friend, Rachel, had said. 'Who'd name a camp after a *tool*?' I had to explain to her that a yellowhammer was a bird.

'Pretty stupid name for a bird, too,' Rachel had said.

She was going to Camp Powhatan with Amanda and the other two members of the Bimbo Brigade: Natalie Smith and Cheryl Ruddick.

I guess you might be wondering why my

sister Amanda and I were going to different camps. Well, I had four good reasons for not wanting to go to Camp Powhatan:

1. Amanda
2. Rachel Goldstein
3. Cheryl Ruddick
4. Natalie Smith

The truth is that Amanda can be OK sometimes. I mean, we get along really well *sometimes*. Like when Amanda isn't trying to be all grown-up and superior and big-headed and know-it-all and treating me like I was some kind of bug that had just crawled out from under a rock.

The thing you have to understand is that Amanda is an *airhead*. Sometimes she's an OK airhead, and sometimes she's a *monster* airhead. It's true. All she's really interested in is boys and trendy clothes and hairstyles and pop singers and movie stars. Now, *sometimes* when the two of us are on our own, Amanda forgets that she thinks she's the most important person in the house, and we get along just fine. But this never, *never* happens when the other three Bimbos are around. When Amanda is with Natalie, Cheryl and Rachel she's a total nightmare.

And that's why I asked Mom and Dad if I could go to a different camp from Amanda.

'I guess you *could* use a rest from each other,' Mom had said. 'OK, you can go to different camps.'

'Hooray!' I yelled. 'Two whole weeks without Amanda!'

'Yah-hoo!' Amanda had hollered. 'Fourteen whole days without Stacy!'

I don't know what *she* was so pleased about. Anyone would think *I* was the family pest, instead of Amanda!

But the thing that made going to camp even *better* was that my friends Fern, Pippa and Andy were able to go to Camp Yellowhammer for the same two weeks.

Andy Melniker is the newest member of our gang, but he fits in really well with the rest of us and we all get along terrifically. Which is odd, because we're all completely different people. Pippa Kane is brainy but a little off-whack most of the time; Fern Kipsak is kind of noisy and really funny, and Andy is . . . well, crazy I guess, although to look at him, you'd think he was totally normal.

But there was a lot of stuff to do before I could go to camp. And a lot of stuff means a lot of lists. I wrote a list of things to take with me. Then I made a list of things I needed to buy. Then I wrote Mom a list of things to do for Benjamin. Benjamin is my cat. He's a Russian Blue, which is a pedigree breed, so he needs special attention.

'Uh-huh?' Mom had said as she'd read my Benjamin list. ' "Play with him at least twice a day. Brush him thoroughly every other day. Try not to let him get up on the roof and chase the birds too often. Change his water regularly." Stacy! I do know how to look after a cat!'

Then I showed Mom my buying list. She crossed some things off and added some things I hadn't thought of.

A few days before we were supposed to go away, I arranged to meet the guys at the mall so we could all do our summer-camp shopping together.

Pippa took charge of all the lists and crossed each item off with a red pen as we bought it.

We were in Molloy's, which is a big department store, and we were at the foot of the escalator, staring up at the floor plan and looking for where they sold suntan lotion and stuff like that.

'Garden equipment – basement,' Fern said. 'Let's go.'

'We're looking for suntan lotion,' I reminded her.

'Exactly,' Fern said. 'People sunbathe in their gardens, don't they?'

'Garden equipment means chairs and parasols and barbecues,' Pippa said.

'And suntan lotion, I bet you,' Fern insisted. 'I'm telling you – people use suntan lotion in the garden.'

'Yeah,' Andy said. 'They also wear *clothes* in the garden, but you wouldn't go down to the garden-equipment department if you wanted a pair of jeans.' He looked at Fern. 'Well, *you* might, but a *regular* person wouldn't.'

'It'll be with the cosmetics,' Pippa said. 'First floor.'

Fern still wasn't convinced, but the four of us headed over to the cosmetics department anyway.

'Well?' Pippa said to Fern, pointing to a whole display of sun creams and sun oils and sunburn lotions.

'Pooh! You just guessed lucky,' Fern said.

The tubes of lotion were divided into numbered racks, from 1 to 15. The higher the number, the better the protection.

'What number do you think we should go for?' I asked.

'How easily do you burn?' asked Andy, reading the label on one of the tubes. 'Do you have sensitive skin? And what does *hypoallergenic* mean?'

We all looked at Pippa. Pippa's mom is a college professor, which meant that Pippa knows a whole lot of words that normal people never get to hear.

'Uh,' Pippa's forehead went all wrinkly, which meant she was thinking. 'It means . . . uh . . . let me see it, Andy.' She took the tube and stared at the writing on the back. 'It means it's really good,' she said at last. '*Hypo*, means very, and *aller* means it's for everyone, and *genic* means good.' She grinned triumphantly. 'That's it!' she said. 'Hypoallergenic means it's very good for everyone.'

'You made that up!' Fern said. 'I bet it doesn't mean anything like that.'

'I bet it does!' Pippa said.

'I bet you a million dollars it doesn't!' Fern said.

'I bet you two million it does!' Pippa said.

'Hey, guys,' said a horribly familiar voice. 'I think we've wandered into the kindergarten by mistake. And they're having an argument about who plays with whose toys.'

I looked around. It was Cheryl. She was

heading towards us with Amanda and the other two Bimbos trailing along behind her.

In case you want to picture them in your mind, I'll just describe the Bimbos. Amanda has blue eyes and blonde wavy hair. I guess you'd call her pretty, although I'd never tell her so. Cheryl has spiky, sticky-up hair and a face like a hyena with stomach cramps. Rachel looks like a gibbon – a really *dumb* gibbon with loads of curly red hair and a skinny, gangly body. Natalie has long ash-blonde hair and a face that always reminds me of a gopher that's just sat on a tack.

They were all carrying shopping bags. I guessed they were doing exactly the same thing as us. It was just our bad luck that we all ended up in the same place at the same time.

Cheryl lifted a bottle of lotion off the rack.

'There you go,' she said with a big smirk. 'It's a special formula for babies and little kiddies. It should suit you guys just fine.'

'Get lost,' I said.

'Are we going to the swimsuit section, or what?' Rachel asked. 'I don't want people thinking we *know* these kids.'

'Just a second,' I said to Amanda. 'What number sun cream should I buy?'

Amanda looked at my face. 'With your complexion,' she said, 'you need a total sunblock. You know what your skin's like – you'll burn to death on the first day.'

She was right. I'd never gotten a tan in my entire life. My skin went from white and freckly to red and peeling after just a couple of minutes in the sun.

The Bimbos went off in search of swimsuits and we chose some tubes of high-protection sun cream and took them to the checkout lady.

We went to Fern's house to double-check that we'd bought everything on our lists.

We emptied our bags out on Fern's bed and our jointly-owned puppy, Lucky, jumped all over our stuff while we were trying to sort it out. Lucky belongs to Fern, Pippa, me and Cindy Spiegel, who was the fourth member of our gang until her whole family moved out to California. Cindy still officially has a twenty-five per-cent share of Lucky, but Andy is kind of looking after her quarter for her.

When we'd finished playing with Lucky we took another look at the brochure for Camp Yellowhammer.

Camp Yellowhammer was brand new. This was its first season. There were lots of pictures in the brochure of wooden cabins and pine trees, and of activities like tennis and volleyball and pony trekking and stuff. The camp was in a valley and it even had a river where you could learn to canoe and life-save and neat stuff like that.

'We could be just like the Harmony Twins in *Spindrift*,' Fern said as we re-read the part about life-saving. (Rebecca and Melissa Harmony were twin lifeguards in *Spindrift*, our favourite soap opera.)

Fern jumped up on her bed and adopted a typical Harmony Twin pose, with her hand shielding her eyes as she scanned the ocean for swimmers in trouble.

Andy went crashing across the bed and grabbed Fern by the leg. She windmilled her arms and fell over while Andy made biting and chewing noises at her ankle.

'What are you *doing*, you idiot?' Fern yelled as Andy started dragging her down the bed.

'I'm a shark,' Andy explained in a raspy, sharky kind of voice.

'Help! Shark attack!' Fern hollered. So Pippa and I jumped on Andy, and then Lucky jumped on all of us, barking like crazy until Fern's mom came up to see what all the noise was about and to tell us that there were some pizza slices heating up in the oven for us.

We were going to have such a brilliant time at Camp Yellowhammer. And best of all, there'd be no Bimbos around to louse things up. It was going to be perfect. I just *knew* it!

Chapter Two

Amanda and I were on the couch in the living room, half-watching television and half-reading our camp brochures for the millionth time. I was explaining about Camp Yellowhammer's river.

'A river?' Amanda said. 'Well, big deal. It says here that Camp Powhatan has a *lake*. And a swimming pool with the longest and highest water slide in the entire state.'

'Huh,' I said. 'I'd prefer a real river to some dumb lake anytime.'

'Will you two quit bickering?' Mom said.

'I'm not bickering,' Amanda said. 'It's Stacy.'

'It is not,' I said. 'Amanda thinks a lake is better than a river.' I looked at my mom. 'Isn't a river better than a lake, Mom? You can do loads more stuff on a river.'

'Yeah,' Amanda said, 'like getting swept

away by the current and never being heard of again. Try it, Stacy.'

'That's enough,' Mom said in her special stern voice.

We sat and read our brochures in total silence for a couple of minutes. Then Amanda gave me a poke with her elbow and pointed to a big picture of the longest and highest water slide in the state. It did look pretty exciting, but I wasn't about to say so to Amanda.

I turned to the page with pictures of people canoeing.

Amanda pulled a face and held her nose.

I stuck my tongue out at her and turned to a page with a picture of a load of people toasting marshmallows around a camp fire.

Amanda shook her head and showed me a picture of Camp Powhatan's disco.

I mimed throwing up.

Amanda started some kind of complicated mime which I couldn't figure out.

'What the heck is that meant to be?' I whispered.

'Me stuffing you in a sleeping bag,' Amanda whispered back, 'dumping you in the river and waving goodbye.'

'Oh, right!' I whispered. 'Check *this* out!' I

mimed tying rocks onto Amanda's feet and throwing her into her precious lake.

'What on earth are you two *doing*?' Mom asked. 'I don't have a family. I have my own private cartoon show!'

Amanda and I looked at each other and burst out laughing.

'Boy,' Mom said, 'am I looking forward to Wednesday!'

Wednesday was when Amanda was going to camp. I was going to Camp Yellowhammer on Saturday. That meant I'd have most of Wednesday and all of Thursday and Friday at home without Amanda to annoy me!

'Are you really looking forward to us going away?' I said, feeling a little offended. 'Don't you like having us around?'

'Sure, I do,' Mom said. 'But I could use a break, too. It'll just be me, Sam and your father. And it'll be so *peaceful*!'

Right at that moment Sam let out a yell from upstairs. Mom sighed and got up.

Amanda grinned at her. 'Yeah,' she said, '*really* peaceful, Mom. I'm just *so* envious!'

* * *

'And keep out of my room, right?' Amanda said as she lugged her duffel bag down the stairs on Wednesday morning. 'My room is totally out of bounds. Got it?'

'Why would I want to go into your room?' I asked as I followed her down.

'To borrow stuff,' Amanda panted as she dragged the bag across the hall. 'You're always borrowing my stuff, and you know it.'

Mom came in through the front door and took hold of Amanda's bulging bag.

'Good grief! From the weight of *this*,' she said with a gasp, 'I shouldn't think there's much stuff left in your room for Stacy to borrow.'

'I've just got the bare essentials,' Amanda said. 'Like you told me, honest. I left loads of stuff out. I don't know *what* I'm going to wear after the first few days.'

'I'm sure you'll be able to wash clothes,' Mom said.

'*Wash clothes*?' Amanda shrieked. 'Mom, are you kidding? This is supposed to be a vacation. I can just see it: "Oh, sorry guys, I can't come to the pool with you today, I've got to do laundry." No way! Cheryl said she's taking a different outfit for every day.'

'Yeah, well, what Cheryl says and what her mom let's her do are two different things,' Mom said. She looked up at me.

'I won't be more than forty-five minutes,' she told me. 'I'll just drop Amanda off at the bus station, pick Sam up from Mrs Lloyd, and I'll be right back. OK, honey?'

'Sure,' I said.

I went to the door. Amanda and Mom carried the bag to the car and heaved it into the boot. The back of the car went down about six inches!

Amanda opened the passenger door. Then she turned and came running up the front path. I was taken by surprise by a hug.

'I'm not going to miss you one little bit!' she said with a big smile.

'Same here,' I said.

We looked at each other.

'Are you going to be OK without me to look out for you?' Amanda said.

'I'll cope,' I said. 'Don't eat any berries you find in the woods. OK? They might be poisonous.'

'Fine. And you watch out for bears and cougars and stuff. I don't want to get home to find you've been chewed up by some wild animals.'

We took another long look at each other.

Mom beeped the car horn.

'*Ciao*, little sister,' Amanda said as she walked down the driveway.

''Bye,' I called. I don't know why, but suddenly I felt kind of fond of Amanda. You know, like I really would miss her.

'And keep out of my room!' Amanda yelled as she climbed into the car. 'Or I'll kill you!'

I waved until the car was out of sight, then I closed the front door and took a deep breath.

Ahh! Three whole days at home without my pesky sister. And then two whole weeks at camp without my pesky sister!

I wandered around the place for a while. I couldn't make up my mind what I wanted to do first.

I could watch television. And there'd be no Amanda sitting there saying, *I don't want to watch this, I want to watch the other channel*. Or I could read without Amanda's music blaring through the wall.

I went upstairs. The house seemed really quiet. I mean, like, *unnaturally* quiet. It was really strange to think that Amanda wouldn't be coming home that night.

I turned the handle of Amanda's door and pushed it open. I know this sounds really stupid, but our house didn't feel *right* without any Amanda-noise in it. Gee, maybe I really would miss her after all.

There was a big sheet of paper on the floor just inside the door. Amanda had written in large red capital letters: *STACY! GET OUT OF MY ROOM!*

Come to think of it, I wasn't going to miss her for one single, solitary *second*!

I slammed the door and went into my own room.

It was a shame she wasn't going away for two *years* instead of only two weeks!

Chapter Three

'And don't forget to yell for him if he doesn't show up for his dinner,' I called to Mom through the open passenger window of the car.

'I won't forget,' Mom called back from the front doorstep.

'And if he doesn't come, he'll either be in the laundry basket or sleeping in my room, OK?' I hollered as Dad started the car.

'Got it,' Mom called.

'And don't give him tins of fishy stuff two day's in a row.'

Mom and our house and everything disappeared around the corner and I slumped into the seat with a sigh.

'I hope he'll be OK without me,' I said.

'I think he'll manage somehow,' Dad said with a grin.

It wasn't a very long drive to the bus pick-up point. The camp bus was due in the town square at ten o'clock in the morning. We'd been told to wait with our things by the fountain opposite the town hall.

The sun was blazing down as Dad parked the car and we headed over to where Pippa and Andy were already waiting with their bags.

'I bet the weather will be like this the whole two weeks!' Pippa said from behind her sunglasses.

'Don't say things like that,' Andy warned her. 'You know what happens when you say things like that!'

He was referring to the Pippa-jinx. If Pippa says something, the exact opposite always happens!

The last thing we needed was for Pippa to make predictions about how great the weather was going to be.

A few minutes later Fern arrived in her dad's car.

'Hi,' I said as she climbed out and yanked out her backpack. 'Do you need a hand with your stuff?'

Fern slung her pack onto the ground.

'This is *it*,' she said. She looked at us. Pippa had three bags. Andy and I had two. Fern had just the backpack.

We all looked at her single, solitary bag.

'What?' she said.

'Do you have enough stuff in there for the whole two weeks?' Pippa asked.

'Sure do,' Fern said with a grin. 'Fourteen pairs of underwear. Fourteen T-shirts and a change of jeans. What else are we going to need?'

The bus came into the square exactly two minutes late, at two minutes past ten. There were already a few people on board but there was still plenty of room – although the back seat had been taken, of course!

We stowed our things and said goodbye to our folks. The bus started up and we were off!

'OK,' Fern said, 'time to 'fess up. Who brought their favourite doll with them?'

'Puh-lease!' I said. 'What are we – babies? All I brought was my lucky pig key-ring. Oh, and a picture of Benjamin.'

'I brought some old comic books,' Andy said.

'You're kind of quiet,' Fern said, looking suspiciously at Pippa. 'What did you bring?'

'Nothing,' Pippa said.

'Huh! Sure!' Fern said. 'Come on, Pippa. You might as well tell us. We'll only go through your stuff at camp otherwise.'

'OK. So I brought Olly,' Pippa said. Olly was Pippa's octopus-shaped pyjama case.

'It was my mom's idea,' Pippa insisted. 'A person can bring a pyjama case with them, can't they?'

We only teased Pippa for a little while. I mean, we were through teasing her by the time we hit the outskirts of town.

'I'm hungry,' Andy said. 'Who has some food?'

Pippa brought out a bag of chocolate-chip cookies which we shared out.

'I've got some candy bars,' Fern said.

'Great!' I said. 'Where?'

'In my pack.'

'You stowed your pack away under the bus,' Andy said.

'Oh, yeah,' Fern remembered. 'Do you think the driver would stop so I could get them?'

'Are you kidding?' Pippa said.

I mean, even Rachel wouldn't ask the driver to pull over in the middle of the highway so she could get some candy bars out of her bag.

'I'll ask him,' Fern said, getting up. We grabbed her and managed to hold her down until she agreed *not* to go and ask the driver to stop.

* * *

We stopped a couple of times at service stations, so we had plenty of snacks and drinks to keep us going, as well as Andy's supply of comic books and some coin tricks that Pippa had learned from a book of one hundred and one coin tricks to baffle your friends and family. Except that the way Pippa performed the tricks, she couldn't have fooled a goldfish!

'The coin is up your sleeve!' I said.

'It is *not*!' Pippa said as the coin fell out of her sleeve and rolled onto the floor of the coach. 'Oh, rats!'

'It's getting kind of cloudy,' Andy said, taking his sunglasses off and peering through the window.

He was right. We were heading towards a huge mass of cloud that stretched clear across the sky from one side to the other.

'Don't worry about it,' Pippa said. 'I bet it's only a thin strip. And they aren't rain clouds, anyway.'

'How can you tell?' I asked.

'Because those clouds are *cirrus* clouds,' Pippa said in her best professor-type voice. 'And rain clouds are *cumulonimbus* clouds. They look totally different.'

'Wow,' Fern said in a very impressed voice, 'Pippa, you are just *so* brainy. So I guess this stuff hitting the window can't possibly be rain.'

It was rain, all right. Huge drops of rain that went *kapow* on the glass and then slid right along sideways.

Pippa leaned across Andy and stared up at the sky.

'Dumb clouds,' she said. 'Quit doing that!'

I laughed. 'Pippa knows they aren't rain clouds,' I said, 'but no one told the *clouds*!'

Five minutes later we were driving through a total rainstorm. And it had become so dark that the driver had to turn the lights on in the bus so we could see what we were doing.

What most of us were doing was staring gloomily out of the windows and hoping Camp Yellowhammer was still a long way away.

'This is all your fault,' Andy said to Pippa. 'I told you not to say it would be sunny.'

'Oh, sure,' Pippa said. 'Like I can change the weather just by *speaking*.'

'If anyone can, it's you,' Fern said. 'Hey, Pippa, I have an idea. Say, "It's going to rain for the next two weeks." That should stop it.'

'Oh, shut up,' Pippa said. 'I'm not going to say another *word*!'

I stared out the window. The rain was bouncing, like, two *feet* off the road and the clouds were so dark that it looked like the middle of the night out there.

'What time were we supposed to get there?' I asked.

'Six o'clock,' Andy said.

'And what time is it now?'

'Do you want the good news or the bad news?' Andy asked.

'The good news,' I said.

'It isn't six o'clock yet,' Andy said.

'And the bad news?'

'It'll be six o'clock in two and a half minutes.'

'Oh, no,' Pippa moaned, putting her hands over her face.

'Maybe we're running real late,' Fern said.

The bus slowed and turned to the right. I looked out the window. I could see that we'd come off the main highway. As I was looking we passed a big, bright, shiny new sign.

CAMP YELLOWHAMMER. ONLY TWO MILES.

'Great!' I said, slumping back in my seat. 'Terrific! Brilliant! Welcome to Camp Yellowhammer, the world-famous underwater summer camp!'

'I guess it was lucky I thought to bring my wet-weather clothes,' Pippa said. 'Hey, guys, why are you looking at me like that? I only said – *yowwlp*!'

We dived on her and spent the last two miles of our trip seeing if her head would fit into the hip pocket of her jeans.

Chapter Four

The bus drove under a cheerful yellow sign. WELCOME TO CAMP YELLOW-HAMMER it said. Perched on one side of the sign was a big carved wooden bird. A yellowhammer, I guess, although for all that I could make out through the pouring rain, it might have been a *duck.*

The bus came to a splashy halt in a big grey parking lot. Through the rain I could see some people scuttling towards us from a long, low cabin. The people were wearing yellow jackets and yellow shorts and were half-hidden under huge yellow umbrellas.

The bus door opened and we all looked at the wet girl who climbed aboard.

'Hi, guys!' she said with a big smile. She was blonde and pretty and so happy-looking that you'd think the sun was blazing down out there. 'Welcome, welcome, *welcome* to Camp Yellowhammer. My name is Marnie, and I'm just one of the camp counsellors who will be looking after you for the next two weeks. And we're all here to make sure that each and every one of you has the very best two weeks of your entire lives!'

We just stared at her while the rain bounced off the coach roof. It sounded like someone was out there throwing rocks down on us.

'I guess you'll all be tuckered out after such a long ride,' Marnie said, 'so we'll get you to your cabins just as soon as you're all registered.'

'*Tuckered out*?' Fern whispered. 'If she doesn't stop smiling like that, I'm gonna scream.'

Marnie's smile *was* kind of overwhelming. It was like having a searchlight in your face.

We started getting off the bus. The other counsellors tried to keep everyone covered by the umbrellas while we dragged our bags out of the stow-hold and made the splashy, splooshy, splodgy run to the main meeting room.

We dumped our bags in the foyer and trudged into a big hall filled with tables and with a platform at one end.

We all sat down and a guy called Brad gave us a welcoming speech and told us not to get downhearted because it was raining. He said this was really *freak* weather around these parts and we should all think positively so that it would be totally sunny and fabulous by tomorrow. Then he told us that dinner was ready.

The cafeteria was a room behind the platform. We stood in line with our trays and pretty soon we were all busy eating.

'This place isn't so bad,' Andy said through a mouthful of brownie.

'I guess not,' Fern said. 'After all, it's only *raining*. I mean, what harm can a little rain do?'

Right on cue all the lights in the hall flickered. Everyone went 'Oooh!' For a few seconds the lights were kind of yellow and feeble, but then they got back to normal.

'It's nothing to worry about,' Brad announced from the platform. 'Everything's OK.'

'Who's worried?' Marnie shouted cheerfully. 'We're not worried, are we, guys?'

'No!' we all shouted, although a few of us didn't sound too sure.

Two seconds later all the lights went out like someone had thrown a switch.

Some of the girls screamed. I didn't scream, although I've got to admit, it was kind of scary. I hadn't realized how dark it was outside.

'No problem!' Brad yelled. 'Just wait up for a few seconds and the auxilliary generators will kick in.'

'How about we all *count* until the lights come back on!' shouted Marnie. 'And then everyone *cheer*!' We counted to one hundred and thirty two. The lights came on and we all cheered.

'A big *hurrah* for the maintenance guys!' Brad said.

After that we finished eating and got registered and allocated cabins. Pippa, Fern and I were in Peewit cabin and Andy was in Jackdaw cabin.

There were telephones in the foyer of the big cabin and most of us called home.

Dad answered the phone. I told him about the rain and he said he'd already heard about it from a weather report on TV.

I checked that Benjamin was OK. Then Dad read out a card they'd just gotten from Amanda.

' "*Dear everyone, camp is great. The weather is great. Having a great time. Love, Amanda.*" '

Great! Amanda *would* have brilliant weather. That was just so totally typical! I was going to spend two weeks under water, and Amanda was going to come home with a golden tan.

The big cabin was in the bottom of the

valley and the cabins where we were going to sleep were on the valley sides. As Marnie led seven of us girls who had arrived on our bus over to Peewit cabin we could see the river pouring down the valley.

'I don't think I want to try canoeing in *that*,' Pippa said. I could see what she meant. The river was racing along really quickly, all white water and full of branches and stuff swept down from higher in the valley.

Not that we spent much time sightseeing right then. Peewit cabin was one of six cabins perched alongside the river. There were bunks for about twenty people in there. Ten were already occupied. I took the bottom of a pair of bunks at the far end of the cabin by the window. Fern had the top bunk, and Pippa's bunk was only a few yards away.

The other girls in the cabin were pretty friendly. There were storage places under the bunks and in big closets. I was just starting to get my stuff out of my bag when Fern said, 'Wow!'

She was sitting on her bunk staring out of the window. I didn't think there was a whole lot to go 'wow!' about out there. Not unless you're really into *rain*.

'Come and look at this, guys,' she said.

We looked out of the window. Down below us we could see the river and the valley bottom and the big cabin.

'Gosh!' Pippa breathed. 'Do you see *that*?'

I sure did. The river was pouring out over its banks. And the flood was getting closer and closer to the big cabin. People were racing around down there, waving their arms in the air and generally looking like they didn't know what to do.

'This vacation could turn out to be really neat,' Fern said. 'Like, an *adventure*!'

I like the idea of adventures as much as the next person, but I kind of like my adventures to be in books or on TV. I like to experience my adventures on a couch at home with a glass of milk and a plate of cookies and Benjamin curled up in my lap.

* * *

According to the brochure, our first night at Camp Yellowhammer was supposed to include a tour of 'the many and varied facilities offered by the camp'. Then there would be a meet-and-greet party in the big cabin where newcomers could get to mix with and make friends with the counsellors. Then, to round our first evening off, there would be a concert party by the counsellors, and 'Barnie Mayfair and his acoustic guitar would perform our favourite songs for a rousing outdoors singalong around a camp fire'. (I don't know how Barnie Mayfair and his acoustic guitar knew what *my* favourite songs were, but I'm just quoting the brochure, OK?)

The brochure lied! We couldn't have been taken for a tour of the many and varied facilities unless we'd been given flippers and snorkels. And by the time Marnie came up to wish us good night, the big cabin was completely surrounded by water. A person would have needed a flame-thrower to try and start a camp fire out there.

I mean, I don't like to be critical, or anything, and I know it wasn't anyone's *fault*, but the way that first night was turning out, I would have had more fun sitting in the bathtub at home and pouring buckets of water over my head.

But like Fern said as the cabin lights went out and we all pulled the blankets up over our ears to try and keep out the endless drumming of the rain on the roof: 'After a start like this,' she said with typical Fern-like confidence, 'things, can only get better!'

Chapter Five

'Whoo! Way to flood the entire camp!'

I was woken by Fern's voice from way up above me. At first I thought I was still at home and that the voice was coming from some kind of strange and undiscovered species of Fern-bird flying around up near my ceiling. (I sometimes think weird things when I'm only just waking up.)

I opened my eyes and remembered where I was. It was morning. A few girls were already up and most of them were staring out of the windows looking more like people about to sit a school test than anything else.

I crawled out of bed and took a look outside for myself. Well, it wasn't raining as hard as it had been last night. That was *something*.

'Hey, look, Stacy,' Fern said. 'We got a *lake*! Just like Amanda's camp!'

I rubbed my eyes and looked again. Fern wasn't kidding. The whole of the valley bottom was one big sheet of brown water. Not only did we have a lake, but we had something that Amanda's camp sure didn't have. We had a lake with a half-sunk cabin in it!

Pippa was sitting on her bunk writing a card.

' "Dear Mom," ' she said aloud as she wrote, ' "we are having some remarkable weather down here. Please send a wetsuit. Glub glub, glub." '

I got dressed and wondered what would happen next. On the other side of the cabin a girl was crying and whimpering about this being the worst vacation of her life. I could understand why she was upset, but the last thing we needed just then was more water!

'Here comes the rescue squad,' Fern said. A bunch of counsellors were squelching their way up the hill towards the six cabins.

Our door opened and a soggy mess came staggering in.

'Hi, everyone,' Marnie said, smiling the kind of smile you see in disaster movies. 'I'm really, really sorry about this, but you're going to have to pack up. The fire department has told us to evacuate the camp.'

'What about breakfast?' someone asked.

'We'll figure something out,' Marnie said.

'It's just that everything's under water down there.'

'Maybe we could have submarine sandwiches,' Fern said. 'Or fish sticks?' No one laughed.

* * *

It took some time to evacuate the camp. We all had to climb up the hill with our bags to where a fleet of buses was waiting for us. Some of the counsellors were busy talking on mobile phones and there were plenty of grown-ups marching around arguing with one another and giving orders.

We met up with Andy and the four of us grabbed the back seat in one of the buses.

'Amazing night, huh?' Andy said. He didn't seem upset about the flood at all. 'Our cabin was making all these creaking noises, like it was about to fall to pieces. Some of the boys in there were total wimps. I tried keeping everyone entertained by telling stories, but a couple of them just totally freaked out.'

'What kind of stories?' Pippa asked.

'Oh, stories about cabins on hillsides in rainstorms,' Andy said, 'and how they come loose from their foundations and go crashing down the hill into deep, dark flood-water so that everyone inside gets drowned. *That* kind of story.'

'Neat,' Fern said with a grin. 'I never expected summer camp to be so exciting. I'm coming here again next year for sure!'

'I don't know what's so darned funny,' Pippa said. She'd slipped in the mud with her three bags and her clothes were kind of yukky. She was still annoyed with Fern because Fern had cracked up laughing instead of helping her up.

'In case you hadn't noticed,' Pippa continued, 'our vacation has been totally ruined! We're all going to be sent straight back home and that'll be *it* for the summer. The closest we're going to get to summer camp now is if we pitch a tent in Stacy's back yard!'

'You shouldn't have said it was going to be sunny!' Fern said, pointing a finger at Pippa.

'Oh, nuts!' Pippa snapped.

'Hi, everyone,' Marnie said from the other end of the coach. 'I've got some really good news for you all. We've been calling around other camps and we've managed to find a camp that's able to take all of you! Now, isn't that something to smile about?'

'So we won't be sent home?' someone asked.

'I'll tell you what the plan is, guys,' Marnie said. 'We're going to drive to town right now, and once we're in town, you're all going to call home to your folks to tell them what happened and to tell them that we've found alternative accommodation for you. And then if any of you want to go home, we'll arrange transportation. But for all of you who still want a brilliant summer vacation, we'll be driving over to another camp.'

'Excuse me,' Fern called. 'What's the weather like at this other camp?'

Marnie laughed. 'It's sunny and warm,' she said.

'Sounds good,' Fern said. 'Let's get rolling!'

I called home from the town, but Mom already knew all about the disaster of Camp Yellowhammer. It had been on the news and everything. In fact, she knew stuff I didn't know. Like the fact that Jackdaw cabin had slid right off its foundations about an hour after the last person had left it and had fallen all to pieces.

Maybe Andy was some kind of psychic. Creepy!

Mom said it was OK for me to go to the other camp, but that I had to call her as soon as I arrived.

'And honey,' she said, 'if you don't like the place they send you, we'll come and pick you up, OK?'

'OK,' I said. 'How's Benjamin?'

'Fine.'

'Is he pining? Is he not eating his food?'

'Nope, he's eating like a horse.'

Well, that was a fine thing. I mean, a person's pampered cat ought to at least look a *little* sad when his beloved owner is away.

Mom put the phone to Sam's ear so I could say hello to him.

'Ugga!' I heard Sam say. 'Ugga Madda!'

Madda was Sam's way of saying Amanda.

'No, Sam.' I said. 'Not Amanda. Stacy!'

'Madda. Madda, Madda!' Sam burbled happily.

Fine! Just fine! Benjamin doesn't miss me at all, and my baby brother thinks I'm my dimwit sister.

It seemed like nearly everyone's parents had already heard about the flood. A few kids were told they had to go straight home (including the girl who'd been blubbing in our cabin) but most of our parents were letting us go on to the alternative camp.

The counsellors bought us some food and

drink for the journey and we all got on board the buses.

* * *

We'd been on the road for a while when Fern said, 'Aw, heck. I've left my candy bars in my bag again!'

We stared at the empty food wrappers and drink cans she'd piled up around her.

'Do you have *room* for anything else?' Pippa asked. We were all pretty much stuffed to bursting point.

'Not right now,' Fern said, patting her stomach. 'But it'd be nice to have the choice in case I get hungry later.'

I'd been keeping an eye on the road signs. We'd been heading north-west on the interstate most of the afternoon. I didn't recognize any of the town names that came up, except for a place called Sullivan, which rang some kind of bell in my head.

'Hey, guys.' I asked as Sullivan got closer. 'Do any of you know why I know that name?'

'Maybe you've been there,' Pippa suggested.

'Nope,' I said. 'It's not that.'

'Maybe you saw it on a map,' Andy said.

'Yeah, maybe.' I said doubtfully. I suddenly sat up. 'Yeah, it was on a map. But not a regular map. It was on a map of how to get somewhere.' I frowned. 'But *where*?'

'Uh-oh! I remember!' Fern said suddenly. 'I saw it at your house, Stacy. Oh, good grief! I don't believe it! I just don't believe this is happening!'

'Tell me,' I said.

'Stacy, believe me,' Fern said. 'You don't want to know.'

I looked at her. 'Will you just tell me?' I said.

Fern shook her head. 'Nope,' she said. 'Because if I do, you'll throw yourself off the bus without waiting for it to stop.'

'Why would she do that?' Pippa asked.

'Because there are some things a person just can't face,' Fern said. She looked at me. 'You still don't remember?'

I screwed my face up and held my breath to try and help me think.

'It was in a booklet,' I gasped. 'Yeah! A booklet or something. It was on the left hand page.' I was trying to picture the booklet in my mind. I could see the map now. It was a simple map, showing the interstate, and showing the turn off for Sullivan. And then the road on the map went past Sullivan and took another turn to . . . to . . .

'AAAAAARRRRRGGGGGHHHHH!!!!!'

'I think she remembered,' Fern said.

'What?' Pippa said. '*What?*'

'Arrrgh!'

'Is it somewhere awful?' Andy asked.

'Arrgh!'

'It must be the worst place in the world!' Pippa said, looking at my face.

'Campawwahharrgghhnnn!' I gabbled.

Pippa blinked at me. 'Say that again?'

'Camp Powhatan!' I yelled at her. 'Camp Powhatan! You come off the interstate, take the road to Sullivan, take a left and you get to Camp Powhatan! That's where we're going. Camp Powhatan!' I put my head in my hands. 'I don't believe it, I don't believe it, I don't believe it,' I moaned.

'Hi, guys,' Marnie said leaning over the backs of the seats and giving us one of her flashlight smiles. 'Is everything okey-dokey back here? Everyone happy?'

I stared at her.

'Can you tell me the name of the camp we're going to?' I asked really slowly. Fingers crossed. Toes crossed.

There might be two summer camps near Sullivan. Yeah, that was it. Two camps. Camp Powhatan and a really nice camp called Camp Notamanda.

A Special Stacy Note

The Notamanda Tribe inhabited the western parts of Indiana. They were a peaceful, intelligent tribe who loved nature and who lived at one with the world. They only had one enemy – the Bimbosi Tribe, led by their fearsome chief *Air in the Head.*

'Sure. I can,' Marnie said with a huge great smile. 'It's called Camp Powhatan.'

'This is a joke, right?' Andy said.

Marnie blinked at him. 'I'm sorry?'

'Stacy's sister is at Camp Powhatan,' Fern explained.

'Well! Won't that be nice!' Marnie said.

Nice? *Nice*?

Two weeks at summer camp with Amanda and the entire Bimbosi Tribe? *NICE*?

Well, excuse me while I throw myself out the window.

Chapter Six

Our convoy of ex-Yellowhammer buses took the left turn after Sullivan and we drove alongside a whole lot of tall fir trees.

'At least it's sunny,' Fern said. She was right there. We were clear of all that freaky weather. We'd left the clouds and the rain miles behind. It was difficult to believe we were still in the same *state*.

The sky was blue except for a few fluffy white clouds, and the sun was so hot that even with the air conditioner on on our bus, it still felt like we were sitting in a microwave.

'If it's a really big camp,' Pippa said hopefully, 'maybe we won't even *see* Amanda and the others.'

'It can't be *that* big,' I said gloomily. 'Nowhere is *that* big.'

Our three buses turned into a tree-lined road and I saw the dreaded sign.

CAMP POWHATAN.

I was surprised that it didn't also say: *Under New Management: this camp is now being run by Amanda Allen and the Bimbo Consortium.*

And then everyone on the bus went 'Whoooooo!' I looked out of the window to see what all the *whooo-ing* was about.

We had driven out of the trees and the whole camp was spread out in front of us. And it sure was worth a *whooo*! It looked really amazing. On one side was a huge lake with canoes and boats and windsurfers on it.

And there must have been about twenty cabins as well as plenty of other wooden buildings, all freshly painted and shining in the sun. And on the far side of the lake was a pool and that water slide that they'd been doing all the boasting about.

'I wanna go on that! I wanna go on that!' Fern gasped, her face *glued* to the window as we headed for the parking area. 'I wanna go on that *right NOW*!'

And there were tennis courts and a baseball diamond and volleyball courts and so much other stuff that it was impossible to take it all in. And the whole place was surrounded by a big forest of fir trees.

'Way to swap camps!' Andy breathed. 'This is, like, Camp Yellowhammer times ten!'

Our buses crawled into the parking lot. There was a bunch of counsellors in brown T-shirts and shorts waving at us as we drove in. And there were plenty of young people hanging around, too. I guess news of the Great Camp Yellowhammer Flood was creating a lot of interest at Powhatan.

The door of our bus hissed open and we fought our way off, just like you have to on a regular school bus.

We finally managed to claw our way out. I was in the mob of people waiting to get their bags out of the side when someone grabbed me from behind and yanked me backwards.

Guess who!

'Amanda! Quit that!' I spluttered with my clothes up around my neck.

'Keep quiet and come with me,' Amanda whispered through clenched teeth.

Some welcome!

Hi, Stacy, I'm so glad you're here safely. Isn't it awful about that flood? Are you OK? They said on the news that half the camp was under water. I was so worried about you. And Cheryl was worried too. We've all been worried sick!

Amanda hauled me around the back of the bus.

'Will you let go of me!' I yelled, glaring at

her. 'I'm just as sick about this as you are! I didn't *volunteer* to come here, you know.'

'Stacy, shush!' Amanda hissed.

She finally let go of me and I was able to straighten my clothes out.

And then she smiled.

'Hi, Stacy,' she said. 'We heard all about the flood. I guess that *would* happen to you, huh?' She smiled a little wider. It reminded me of Marnie's smile when she'd come into the cabin to tell us we needed to get out of there. It was a weird kind of smile. Like, her *mouth* was smiling, but the rest of her face wasn't in on the act, if you see what I mean.

'Can I go get my bags?' I asked.

'In one minute,' Amanda said. 'I need to talk to you first. I need . . . I . . . uh . . . oh, heck!'

Suddenly Amanda's smile looked even more desperate.

'What?' I asked.

'If I was in real big trouble,' Amanda said, grabbing hold of my shoulders and bringing her face right up close to mine. 'If I was in awful trouble, you'd help me out, wouldn't you, Stacy?'

'Sure,' I said, jerking my head back as her nose almost jabbed me in the eye.

She let out a relieved breath. 'Then you'll back me up, huh?'

'I guess so,' I said uncertainly. 'Back you up with *what*?'

Amanda glanced around like a secret agent in a spy movie.

Amanda Bond: Licensed to Annoy.

'I don't have time to tell you right now,' she said. 'All you need to remember is that your name is Laine and that we live in Beverly Hills.'

'*What*?'

'Don't ask why, Stacy,' Amanda said. 'Just *do* it, please.'

'Now, wait a minute.'

'And we've got an older sister called Stacy,' Amanda gabbled at me, still glancing around every which way as if she was sure someone would be listening. 'And she's an actor, right? And she's gong to be starring in her own TV series, OK? Called *Stacy, Stacy*.'

'What the heck have you been *telling* people?' I gasped. 'Amanda, I can't back you up on stuff like *that*!'

'You've got to!'

'No way!'

'But I'll just *die*!'

'So, *die*,' I said, 'I'm not doing it, OK?'

'You can't do this to me!' Amanda collapsed onto her knees in front of me, her hands holding my wrists really tightly. She looked up at me like a spaniel begging to be forgiven. You know the kind of expression I mean. All huge eyes and pleading looks.

'Please back me up!' she said. 'Please, please back me up! Pleasepleasepleaseplease-please!'

'Amanda!'

But she just kept right on going *pleaseplease-please* over and over again.

'OK, *OK!*' I said. I had to shut her up somehow. 'I'll do it! I'll *do* it!'

Amanda jumped to her feet and gave me a smothering hug.

'Thankyouthankyouthankyou,' she burbled. 'You've got no idea how important this is to me.'

'Get out of here,' I said, pushing her away. I gave her a stern look. 'OK,' I said, 'here's the deal. I'll back you up *for the time being*. But I want a really good explanation right?'

'Right!' Amanda said. 'No problem. I'll explain everything. And it's not as bad as it sounds, Stacy, honest it isn't.'

'It had better not be,' I said. 'Because from

where I'm standing it sounds like you've turned into some kind of total *fib-machine*!'

'Just stand by me for the time being,' Amanda said. 'And if you don't approve when I tell you the whole story later, you can make your own mind up what to do, OK?'

'Hmmm,' I said. (I sounded pretty much like my mom with that *hmmm*. Mom does really good *hmmms* when a person is about to explain how a vase got broken or why there's blueberry jam down the back of the television set. And judging by what Amanda had just been saying, I was in for a pretty whacky explanation.)

'And watch out for a girl called Andrea, OK?' Amanda warned me. 'Andrea Wolfson.'

'OK, message received,' I said. 'Can I go get my bags now, before the bus drives away with them?'

Pippa had taken my bags off the bus and she and Fern and Andy were standing looking around in a puzzled way.

'There she is!' Pippa said as Amanda and I came around the side of the bus. 'Oh, hi, Amanda.'

'Hi, guys.' Amanda said.

'We're supposed to be going over there,'

Andy said, pointing to the nearest building. 'We've got to get registered and stuff.'

'I'll come with you,' Amanda said. 'I can show you the ropes.' She looked at me. 'Do you want to tell them your new name?'

Andy, Pippa and Fern looked at me.

'Uh, just for *now*,' I said, feeling kind of silly, 'I'd like you to call me *Laine*. Not Stacy. Laine.'

'Why?' Fern asked.

'Because it'll be fun,' Amanda chipped in.

'It will?' Pippa said. 'In what way?'

'In a *fun* way,' Amanda said. 'Could you just *do* it, please?'

I looked at my friends and shrugged. 'Just call me Laine for *now*, right? Amanda is going to explain *why* real soon.'

'Fine by me,' Fern said, picking up her bag and heading towards the registration hut. 'I'll call you anything you like,' she called back. 'I'll call you Peaseblossom Pandabody if you like.'

She would, too!

'Laine will be just fine, thanks,' I said as the rest of us followed her up the path to the glass doors of the hut.

There were plenty of people milling around in there. Amanda kept herself *glued* to me all the time, and she was constantly looking over her shoulder. It was like I was some VIP and she was my bodyguard, ready at a split-second's notice to leap on anyone who came near me.

'Don't forget to tell them you're *Laine*,' she whispered as it came to my turn to get registered.

'Name, please?' asked the man at the desk.

'Laine Allen,' I said.

He frowned. He ran his finger down a row of names on a sheaf of paper. 'We have a *Stacy* Allen on the list,' he said. 'But no Laine.'

I heard Amanda groan.

'That's me.' I said. 'I have two different names.' I smiled at him. 'Sometimes I'm Laine and sometimes I'm Stacy, but they're both me. At the moment I'm Laine.'

'No problem,' said the man, crossing out Stacy and writing in Laine and then ticking my name off. 'You're in Wampum cabin. You'll find directions on the map. Have a nice stay at Camp Powhatan, Laine.'

Amanda and I waited while the others got themselves sorted out. Fern and Pippa were in the same cabin as me again, and Andy was in Lakota cabin.

I made a quick call home to say where I

was. For some reason my dad just started *yelling* with laughter when I told him how I'd ended up at Amanda's camp. *I* don't know what was so darned funny.

And then Amanda spoke to him and told him how she'd joined the camp cheerleading squad and was teaching them some new routines. And then she said something about looking after me, which was a *real* joke!

A counsellor was at the exit, welcoming people all over again and telling them to dump their gear in their cabins and then meet up for a *powwow* at Beaver cabin in half an hour.

There was another welcoming committee waiting for us out in the sunshine of Camp Powhatan. They were standing there in T-shirts and shorts and sunglasses and big smiles. The Bimbo Triplets!

'Hi, Sta – ow!' Cheryl elbowed Rachel in the ribs halfway through her calling me *Stacy*.

'Hi, Cheryl,' I said. 'Hi, Rachel. Hi, Natalie.'

'Hi, Laine,' they chorused. 'Hi, Pippa. Hi, Fern. Hi, Andy.'

'I think I'm going to throw up,' Fern said.

'Let's help these guys with their bags,' Amanda said.

'Sure thing,' Cheryl said.

'I *am* going to throw up,' Fern said as our bags were taken and we were led to our cabins.

We reached Andy's cabin first.

'Meet up with us over by the lake,' I told him. 'Then we can *all* enjoy Amanda's explanation of why I'm called *Laine*, and how come I've got a big sister called *Stacy*.'

Andy, Pippa and Fern stared at me.

I didn't blame them!

Chapter Seven

'Run that past me again,' Pippa said.

I explained exactly what Amanda had said.

Fern stared at Amanda. 'Boy, have you been telling some whoppers!'

'It's not like that at all,' Amanda said. 'I'll explain everything. Just – oh! Oh, *heck*!' Amanda was looking right past me. I looked around.

A girl was heading our way. I guess she was about Amanda's age. She has masses of chestnut-brown hair that bounced and flowed as she moved, just like hair does in shampoo commercials.

'It's Andrea Wolfson,' Amanda hissed right in my ear. 'Remember what I told you! Play it cool!'

I could see why Andrea Wolfson was Amanda's big problem in Camp Powhatan. She was at least as pretty as Amanda, with cheekbones that could cut glass and big, blue eyes. And she had a great figure under really tight shorts and T-shirt. *And* she had bigger boobs than Amanda!

But there was something about the expression on her face that I didn't really like. A snooty kind of look, like there was a permanent bad smell under her nose.

She came strolling up, looking at us like we were exhibits in a freak show.

'Is this place a dump, or what?' she said in a voice which made me think of a dentist's drill. 'I've just been to the camp leisure co-ordinator to ask why there's no jacuzzi. I mean, can you *believe* it? Are we in the twentieth century here, or what?' She stared at us. 'Oh, I guess you'll be the refugees from the camp in the swamp.' She tossed her hair. 'I guess the counsellors must know what they're doing, allowing a whole *army* of people to just walk right in here. I just hope they remember that *we* were here first when things start to run out.'

Nice girl!

'This is my sister, Laine,' Amanda said putting her hand on my shoulder. 'And her friends, Pippa, Fern and Andy.'

'You people look a total mess,' Andrea said.

'Didn't you have time to clean up after you all got wet?'

'We have cleaned up,' Fern said crossly.

'Well, sorr-ee!' Andrea said. 'I saw your awful clothes and I naturally assumed you'd been given them by some kind of disaster relief charity. Still,' she shrugged, 'maybe the hobo look is all the rage in California right now.'

'Excuse me, in *where*?' Andy asked.

'Well, as you're all friends, I kind of assumed you all came from the same place as Amanda,' Andrea said.

'They do,' Amanda said. 'We're all from Los Angeles, aren't we, guys?'

'Sure thing,' I said before anyone had the chance to blow it.

'Well, I guess *some* people must like living on the west coast,' Andrea said. 'But I find that most people with good taste prefer New York. It's so much less *fake*, don't you think? Mommy and Daddy and I live in this totally *huge* hotel in New York. We rent a whole floor. I mean, I wouldn't live in California if you *paid* me. The place is totally gross.'

'I think we'd better get over to your cabin, guys,' Amanda said. 'We'll catch up with you later, Andrea, OK?'

'Yeah, I guess you will,' Andrea drawled.

'Unless my *reprieve* comes through.' She gave us another one of her sour looks. 'I mean, I know Mommy said it would do me good to mix with ordinary people, but I think she kind of lost the plot when she sent me here. I mean, there's ordinary and there's *ordinary*, huh? But I guess you guys understand what I mean.' She stared straight at me. 'Living in a mansion in Beverly Hills and everything,' she said. 'I mean, *we* only have seventeen rooms and four guests suites.'

'Come on, guys,' Amanda said, herding us away from Andrea. 'Let's get you settled in.'

I felt kind of shell-shocked by Andrea, and if the looks on their faces were anything to go by, so did Andy, Pippa and Fern.

Amanda pointed Andy towards Lakota cabin. We arranged to meet up with him a little later, and the rest of us set off for Wampum cabin.

'Who the heck is *she*?' Fern asked as Amanda and the others led us into our cabin. 'The winner of Miss Teenage Ego-trip, or what?'

'*That*, was Andrea Wolfson,' Natalie said, as if her name tasted bad.

'She's a total liar,' Rachel said. 'I mean, like

I really believe her folks rent the entire floor of a New York hotel!'

'So, she's the reason you've been telling all these *gluumph*!' I was stopped in mid-sentence by Amanda's hand over my mouth.

I glanced around. There were a couple of girls over at the far end of the cabin. They were looking at us. I guess Amanda didn't want to discuss this *thing* she had with Andrea Wolfson where anyone could overhear her.

But I was already beginning to understand why Amanda had a problem with Andrea. She was a total monster!

Mind you, I still needed a good explanation for how come I was *Laine*, and how come we were all supposed to be living in mansions in Beverly Hills. It sounded to me like Amanda had gone a little crazy with the exaggerations.

'Just dump your bags and let's go somewhere more private,' Amanda said softly. 'And then I'll tell you the whole story.'

We met up with Andy by the lake. He was watching some people being taught how to do kayak rolls in the shallows.

'OK,' I said, turning to Amanda. 'Spill the beans. What have you been telling people? And this had better be good.'

'It is,' Cheryl said.

We all sat down in the grass.

'Rachel started it,' Amanda said.

'I did not!' Rachel yelled. 'It was Natalie.'

'Wait a minute,' Natalie squeaked. 'All I said was that we'd shut Andrea up if we said we came from somewhere really cool, like Los Angeles.' She pointed at Rachel. 'It was *you* who said we all lived in Beverly Hills.'

'Well, yeah,' Rachel admitted. 'But I had to say something, and I don't *know* any other parts of Los Angeles. Beverly Hills is the only place I've *heard* of.'

'But what's this got to do with Stacy having to be known as *Laine*?' Pippa asked.

'Well,' Amanda began really slowly, 'when we told Andrea we all lived in Beverly Hills, she said, "Do you know anyone famous?" And I said, uh . . . well, I said we lived on the same street as Dynamo Duke Logan.'

Dynamo Duke Logan was the hottest action-movie star in the entire country. I mean, he was mega-big!

'Are you crazy?' I said. 'I've seen a picture of the place where he lives. It's bigger than the whole of Four Corners!'

'I know,' Amanda admitted. 'And I wouldn't have said it if Andrea hadn't been boasting her head off about meeting Crystal van Diamond at a fashion show that her *mother* was putting on in Manhattan.'

Crystal van Diamond was fashion model *numero uno.* There was a competition going around right then where you could win a prize if you could find a fashion magazine that *didn't* have her face on its front cover.

'Yeah, right!' Cheryl said. She looked at me. 'Don't you see the problem, Stacy? Andrea was driving us all nuts with her big-head stories. There's no way even half of what she says can be true!'

'So you thought you'd make up some even wilder stuff, huh?' Andy said. 'I guess I can understand that.'

'Will someone please explain why I need to be called *Laine*?' I said.

'Because I told Andrea that my sister Stacy was an actor,' Amanda said.

'And Andrea said, "So, what's she appeared in that I might know?" ' Cheryl said.

'She said it in the kind of way that means, "If *I* don't know it, it isn't worth knowing," ' Natalie chipped in.

'And I said, she's only had bit parts so far,' Amanda continued. 'And Andrea went, "Oh, *right.*" '

'She says "Oh, right" in a really annoying way,' Rachel added.

I could believe that!

'So, I said she was about to get her first big break,' Amanda said. 'I told her that my sister Stacy was about to star in her own TV series called *Stacy, Stacy*.'

'And that shooting was starting any day now,' Natalie added. 'Which was why Stacy couldn't be *here*.'

'Excuse me,' Pippa said. 'Can I just check that I'm following all this? You *all* live in Beverly Hills, right, and Stacy is going to be a TV star?' She pointed at me.

'No, no, no,' Amanda said. 'Not *Stacy*. Stacy is *Laine*. That's the whole point. Stacy can't be *Stacy*, because Andrea thinks *Laine* is Stacy.'

'Andrea thinks Laine is Stacy?' Fern repeated slowly. 'But you said *Stacy* is *Laine*. I mean. Andrea *thinks* Stacy is Laine.'

'Look,' Cheryl said. 'It's really simple. Amanda told Andrea that their cousin Laine was her sister Stacy, and when Andrea asked who Stacy was, Amanda couldn't say *she* was Stacy as well, so she told her that Stacy was Laine. What's so complicated about that?'

Fern made burbling noises and wobbled her fingers over her rubbery lips.

'Show them the picture, Amanda,' Natalie said.

'Of course,' Amanda said. 'The *picture*!' She leaned over and pulled a slightly crumpled photograph out of the back pocket of her shorts. She handed it to me.

It was a picture of Amanda and me and our eighteen-year-old cousin, Laine Shelby Baxendale. Laine is really gorgeous. The kind of gorgeous that Amanda desperately wants to be. Blonde and curvy and totally grown-up and sophisticated.

'Andrea wanted to know what Stacy looked like,' Amanda explained. 'And this was the only picture I had on me.'

'I get it!' I said. 'You told Andrea that Laine was *me*. That Laine was *Stacy*.'

'That's right,' Amanda said.

I frowned. 'Hey, wait a minute. Why couldn't you just have said *I* was me. Why did you have to tell her Laine was me?'

'Uh, I don't remember too well,' Amanda said evasively.

'Sure you do, Amanda,' Rachel said. 'Don't you remember? When you showed Andrea the picture, she went, "Ew! Who's the geek with the brace and the freckles?" and you said, "That's my little sister, Laine," Remember?'

Amanda glared at her, 'Oh, yeah,' she said. 'Thanks a lot, Rachel.'

'She called me a geek?' I said.

'Be honest,' Natalie said. 'You do look a *little* geeky.'

'WHAT?'

'In the picture! In the picture!' Natalie babbled. 'It's just the *smile* that does it. I don't mean you look geeky in real life.'

'Of course not,' Cheryl said. 'I mean, looks like yours will be all the rage . . . uh, one day . . .'

'I do not look like a *geek*!' I yelled.

'OK! Calm down, Stacy,' Amanda said.

'You mean, *Laine*,' Rachel giggled.

'Oh, shut up, Rachel,' Amanda snapped.

There was silence for a few moments.

Fern leaned over my shoulder and took a long look at the picture.

'You do look kind of geeky,' she said. I think she could tell by my expression that I wasn't too pleased with her. 'In a really nice way,' Fern added. 'A tiny bit geeky in the cutest possible way.'

'I'd quit right now, Fern,' Andy said. 'Before she *kills* you.'

'So,' I said when I'd finished glaring at Fern, 'Laine is our big sister, right?'

'Absolutely!' Amanda said.

'And we live in Beverly Hills, a few mansions down the street from Dynamo Duke Logan. And right this minute, Laine is shooting a TV series.'

'Totally correct,' Amanda said.

'And Andrea Wolfson actually *believes* all this?'

'She does so far,' Cheryl piped up. 'I mean, come on. You don't know the kind of stuff she's been telling *us*!'

'But what if Andrea is telling the truth about herself?' Pippa asked.

'What?' Natalie said. 'That she lives in a zillion-room apartment in the middle of New York? That her dad is some kind of hot-shot, trouble-shooting, international diplomat kind of a guy who advises the president and everything?'

'And that her mom is an Olympic athlete,' Cheryl said, 'who owns a chain of clothes stores and markets her own brand of perfume in her spare time? Puh-lease! The girl is a total liar.'

'But you're lying right back!' I said. 'What's the difference?'

'The difference is that we're nice people,' Amanda said, 'and Andrea Wolfson is a lying sleazeball.' She looked hopefully at me. 'You don't have to make any stuff up,' she said. 'You may not even have to speak to her. All I'm asking is that you don't give the game away if she says anything to you. That's not too much to ask.'

'I'm up for it,' Fern said. 'Andrea is obviously a total creep. I'm going to say I own a beach house and that I spend all my free time surfing the big breakers!'

'She'll wonder how come you don't have a tan,' Andy said.

Fern shrugged. 'I'll tell her the only free time I get is at night,' she said.

'I don't want to have to try and make stuff up,' Pippa said. 'I'm really bad at lying. But I'll go along with it if Stacy will.'

'Count me in,' Andy said. 'It sounds like it could be fun.'

'Stacy?' Amanda asked. 'Please? Pretty please?'

'I need to think about it,' I said. 'If Andrea Wolfson is *really* as bad as she seemed at first sight, then I guess she deserves it.' I gave Amanda a hard look. 'But what if she finds out that we're making it all up?'

'She won't if we all get our stories straight and stick together,' Amanda said.

I shook my head. It sounded really risky to me. The risk being that Andrea Wolfson would be able to prove that the whole bunch of us were lying like crazy. And then where would we be?

I'll tell you where we *wouldn't* be. We wouldn't be living a couple of mansions down the hill from Dynamo Duke Logan, that's for sure! The whole bunch of us would be in Dumpsville for the next two weeks!

Chapter Eight

Things got kind of hectic after our little discussion with Amanda and her idiot friends. Pippa pointed out that we were late for the official welcome in Beaver cabin.

'Back me up, huh?' Amanda called as the four of us skedaddled over to the welcome meeting. 'Stacy? I'll never ask you for anything ever again.'

'I'll think about it,' I called back. 'I've got to decide what it's *worth*.' You should have seen the look on Amanda's face! She couldn't decide whether to get down on her knees and beg, or dump me in the lake.

'You can't really hand Amanda over on a plate to that Andrea Wolfson girl,' Fern said as we made our way through the doors of Beaver cabin. 'She's a total creep.'

'Yeah,' I agreed. 'But *Beverly Hills*! Movie-star neighbours! A sister with her own TV series! Why couldn't Amanda have made up something at least halfway believable! I don't know thing *one* about any Hollywood stuff.'

'Sure, you do,' Fern said. 'Think *Spindrift*. The Harmony Twins live in Beverly Hills. Think like a Harmony Twin.'

Beaver cabin looked like it doubled as a gym. We sat on the polished wooden floor while a couple of counsellors ran through the kind of activities the camp provided.

One big thing that was coming up soon was an Open Day. It was a day when we could invite our folks over to the camp to take a look around and to have a picnic by the lake and watch a special show with a rock band and a stand-up comedian and other neat stuff.

One of the counsellors made a joke about the weather being a whole lot more predictable around here.

'And rest assured, guys,' said the counsellor, 'in Camp Powhatan *you* have to go to the lake. The lake doesn't come to *you*.'

We also found out how come the camp had been able to take all of us. Six new cabins had been built, which weren't expected to be ready for use for another month. But they had been finished early, so they'd just been standing empty. Lucky, huh? Except that it would have been a whole lot *more* lucky if it had been a *different* camp. A camp without a certain big sister with an over-active imagination.

After the welcome in Beaver cabin, we were taken to the Chuckwagon, which was what they called the cafeteria.

After we'd eaten, we chatted with some counsellors and signed up for some activities before going back to our cabins and crashing out. I think I was asleep before my head even hit the pillow. It had been one *long* day.

* * *

We were woken up by Native-American drums being played over the PA system and a voice telling us that it was going to be another brilliantly sunny day.

We had to postpone our ride on the water slide. We spent the morning over by the lake. We were organized into small groups with a counsellor each and then we were told all the *do*s and *don't*s of activities which involved deep water.

'I think the basic rule is, *don't drown*,' Andy said to me as we sat on a wooden jetty watching two counsellors life-save each other.

We were shown how to get in and out of a kayak. Pippa fell in. (I mean she fell in the *lake*, not the kayak.) We were even shown how to roll the kayaks all the way over and come up again.

I was a little nervous when it came to my turn, but there was a counsellor in the water right beside me. I took a deep breath, like they'd told us, and flipped my kayak over. There were a few seconds of rushing and bubbling water and then I was up in the sunlight again and feeling really pleased with myself.

After lunch Fern and Andy went for tennis coaching and Pippa and I joined a bunch of people on a nature trail through the woods.

We were given drawing paper and lists of bugs and plants to look for which we ticked off as we went along.

I had a really great time. I love nature and wildlife and stuff like that, and by the time we got back I had a whole bunch of sketches of leaves and beetles and flowers.

We met up with Andy and Fern in the Chuckwagon. It was so noisy that you almost had to yell to make yourself heard.

We found four seats together. One thing was for sure, with all us Yellowhammer refugees in the place, it was kind of crowded in there at meal times.

'Did you know that shieldbugs are more

commonly known as stinkbugs because they give off an unpleasant odour when disturbed?' I said, reading from one of the leaflets we'd been given during the afternoon. 'The smell comes from things called *stink glands* situated near their hind legs.'

'No, I didn't,' Fern said through a mouthful of hot dog. 'Thanks for telling me while I'm *eating*, Stacy.'

'This potato salad smells kind of strange,' Andy said, poking at it with his fork. 'Hey, what colour are stinkbugs?'

Fern stopped with her fork halfway in her mouth and a really anxious expression on her face.

'The ones that live on plants are green,' Pippa said. 'And the ones that live on trees are brown. It's camouflage, see?'

'Uh-oh,' Andy said. 'I think I'll pass on the potato salad.'

Fern emptied her mouth into a napkin and stared at Andy's plate.

'Did you find a bug?' she whimpered.

Andy grinned at her. 'Nope,' he said.

'What!' she yelled. 'So what was all that about passing on the potato salad?'

'I just remembered I don't like potato

salad,' Andy said. 'Why? What did you think I meant?'

'You know darned well what I thought,' Fern growled.

While we were eating we wrote out a few postcards. One of the cards I wrote was to my pen pal Craig. Craig is really into astronomy – you know, stars and constellations and stuff like that.

I knew he'd be interested that one of the planned activities later on in the week was going to be an open-air night-time talk on stars.

'I bet we'll be able to see *thousands* of stars way out here in the country,' I said to the others. 'You can always see more stars out of town.'

'Yeah,' Fern said. 'Big thrill.'

'Did you know,' Pippa said in her professor voice, 'that if you stand at the bottom of a deep well and look up, you can see the stars even if it's the middle of the day?'

'Get out of here!' Andy said.

'It's true,' Pippa insisted. 'I read it in an encyclopedia. The sky looks black and you can see stars.'

'What?' said a voice like a dentist's drill. 'Stars like Dynamo Duke Logan?'

We looked around. In all the noise and bustle, no one had noticed Andrea Wolfson standing right behind me. She was *just* the kind of person who'd listen in on other people's conversations.

'No,' I said, 'stars like Betelgeuse and Rigel and Sirius. We were talking about *astronomy*, actually.'

'Oh, right,' Andrea said. 'Daddy was really into astronomy a few years back. He had his own observatory and everything. He even found a new star that no one had ever seen before.' She smiled smugly. 'He registered it in my name. There's a star out there called Andrea Wolfson.'

'Oh, sure!' Fern said. 'I really believe that stars get named after *people*.'

'They do, actually,' I said. I didn't like having to back Andrea up, but I remembered Craig telling me that if a person discovered a new star, they could give it any name they liked.

'I thought everyone knew *that*,' Andrea said, giving Fern a really deadly look. 'Don't they teach you anything where you come from?'

'For your information,' Fern said, 'we go to the same school as Ashley Mercury.'

I gave Fern a nervous look. Ashley Mercury was a boy star who was earning mega-million bucks just then. He had become an instant hit when he'd been eight years old. He'd appeared in a movie called *Momma's Little Helper*. It was a really funny film, and there'd been sequels called *Daddy's Little Helper* and *Grandpa's Little Helper*.

'Oh, really?' Andrea drawled. 'I thought I read that he had, like, his own private tutor.'

'Only when he's working on a movie,' Andy said. 'The rest of the time he goes to a regular school, just like anyone else.' He gave Andrea a big smile. 'He's a really nice guy.'

I glanced up at Andrea, trying to figure out whether she had swallowed the story. I mean, if she believed we attended the same school as Ashley Mercury, then she'd believe *anything*!

'It must be a real drag having to put up with shutterbugs and reporters following you around everywhere you go,' Andrea said.

'Shutterbugs?' Andy said. 'Are they anything like stinkbugs?'

'I meant *photographers*,' Andrea sighed, as though we were the dumbest bunch of people in the entire world.

'They don't follow us around,' I said. 'They only follow famous people.'

'But your sister Stacy is famous,' Andrea

said. 'I would have thought they'd want to interview you. To get the inside story on what it's like to have a TV star for a sister.'

'They haven't yet,' I said.

Andrea gave me a long, hard look. I just wished I could figure out what she was thinking!

'So,' she said, 'what *is* it like having a famous sister?'

I shrugged. 'She's not so famous,' I said.

'I think I'd be totally jealous,' Andrea said. 'Except that I don't have any brothers or sisters, so who knows, huh?' She looked around at the four of us. 'Mommy took a break of a whole year in her career to have me. You'll have heard of my mother, of course. Tasmin Wolfson.'

'Uh, who?' Fern asked.

'Tasmin Wolfson,' Andrea said. 'The *swimmer*. She was in all the papers a few years ago. She was supposed to be on the Olympic swimming team, but she had to drop out because her business commitments meant she couldn't give one hundred per-cent to the team. Mommy has to give one hundred per-cent to everything.' She flicked her hair over her shoulder. 'I'm *just* like her in that respect.' She gave me a really *strange* look.

'I guess you know all about commitment, huh, Laine?' she said. 'I mean, your sister Stacy must have worked like crazy to get to where *she* is.'

'You know how it is,' I said. 'Some people have it and some people don't.'

Andrea nodded. 'Yeah, right. Uh, Amanda never *did* tell me what line of work your folks are in.' She leaned closer to me. 'I mean, they must have, like, totally *fabulous* jobs to be able to afford to live in the same street as Duke Logan.'

Uh-oh! This was it! This was the moment I'd been dreading. Either I did some mega-quick thinking or I blew Amanda's whole story wide open.

Stacy Allen, your big moment has arrived. You're appearing on everyone's favourite game show: Truth or Dare! Everyone is rooting for you, Stacy. Or should I say, Laine? Which is it to be? Stacy Straight-arrow or Forked-tongued Laine? The choice is yours!

Gee, thanks!

Chapter Nine

Amanda, one day I really will *kill* you!

I could tell that Pippa and Fern and Andy were staring at me just as hard as Andrea was. It seemed like *everyone* was waiting for me to tell her what my mom and dad did for a living.

What do I do? What do I SAY?

And then it happened. I came up with an idea.

'My mom works with scripts,' I said, 'and my dad sells stories.'

Andrea blinked at me, as if she was trying to figure out exactly what I meant.

'Oh, *film* scripts?' she said.

'Are there any other kind?' I asked with a big grin. Then I remembered my brace and stopped grinning.

'So your mother writes film scripts and your father sells them to movie studios, huh?' Andrea said. 'I guess they must be really successful, huh?'

'I suppose so,' I said.

'So, tell me,' Andrea said. (That girl was determined to give me a grilling!) 'What films have they worked on?'

'Did you see *Unconditional Surrender*?' I asked.

Andrea's eyes narrowed to little slits.

'Ye-e-esss,' she said. 'Are you telling me your mom *wrote* that?'

'Well,' I said. 'Someone's got to do all the hard work behind the scenes.'

'Well, yeah,' Andrea said, doing her best not to look too impressed. 'They wanted my mother to appear in a movie, but she turned it down.' She gave a tight little smile. 'She didn't like the script. Gee, I hope it wasn't one of your mom's scripts.'

'I don't think so,' I said. 'None of my mom's scripts has ever been turned down.'

STACY'S CONSCIENCE TO STACY: Uh, could I butt in for a moment here Stacy? I couldn't help noticing that you're doing some pretty heavy *lying*. Are you sure you feel *good* about this?

STACY TO CONSCIENCE: I haven't told one single lie!

CONSCIENCE: Well, excuse *me*, but this is the first that I've heard about your mom writing film scripts! Or that your dad sells them, for that matter.

STACY: I never said they *did*. I said my mom works with scripts. She does. She proof-reads book manu-*scripts*. And my dad sells books, right? And don't books have stories in them? I never said they were *film* scripts or film *stories*. Andrea just kind of *assumed* they were. Is it my fault if Andrea assumes things wrong?

CONSCIENCE: Uh, I'll tell you what, Stacy. I'll just sit quietly in a corner and keep my mouth shut. How does that sound to you?

STACY: Thanks, Conscience. That sounds just fine. And, hey, you're doing a great job!

Stacy and her amazing brain had done it again! I'd managed to convince Andrea that my folks were knock-'em-dead film people without actually *saying* so at all.

And the last thing I'd said was true as well. None of my mom's scripts *had* been turned down. Mainly because she'd never written any! Sneaky, or what?

'So, your mom could have been a film star, huh?' Fern said. I recognized the tone in her voice. It meant: In a pig's eye!

'Uh-huh,' Andrea said. 'She was cast as a girl who'd been lost in the African jungle as a child and brought up by wild animals. They wanted someone totally athletic and stunningly beautiful and awesomely talented. And Mommy was, like, the only person on the list! But she said, *no way*, not for a measly six million dollars.'

'What's this film called?' Pippa asked.

'*Wolfgirl*,' Andrea said.

'Never heard of it,' Fern said.

'No, of course not,' Andrea said without batting an eyelid. 'The whole thing fell through when Mommy said she couldn't do it. I mean, like, the whole film was written with her in mind, you know?'

'Boy,' Andy said, 'your mom must have been *really* busy to turn down a chance like that!'

'I think *I* was part of the reason,' Andrea said. 'I was going through a really, really important phase in my training, and Mommy just had to be there to cheer me on.' She looked around at us. 'You know what moms are like.'

'What were you training to be?' I asked.

'A swimmer, just like Mommy,' Andrea said. She gave a toss of her hair. 'A couple of members of the Olympic selection team have been kind of hanging around at the private pool where I train. They think I could be even better than Mommy.' She shrugged. 'But, I don't know. I'd kind of like to travel the world and *live* a little, you know? Training is *such* a drag, even when you're a total *natural* like me. But I don't know if I can just turn my back on it all when Mommy and Daddy have spent a *fortune* on my own private swimming coach.'

'Yeah, I know what you mean,' Fern said. 'Don't you just hate letting people down like that? Especially when they've spent a *fortune*!' Then she started laughing, which she quickly turned into a coughing fit.

Pippa thumped Fern on the back while Andrea stared at her as if she was looking at some kind of insect that had just crawled onto the table.

But if Andrea was making all this stuff up as she went along, she had to be the best storyteller since Hans Christian Andersen! No wonder Amanda and the Bimbos had gone ballistic trying to keep up with her.

Then Andrea looked back at me.

'You know, it's kind of *strange*,' she said. 'You guys just don't behave the way I'd expect Beverly Hills people to behave.'

'Uh, how's that?' I asked. I didn't like the way the conversation was going.

'Excuse me,' Andy butted in. 'I don't want to sound rude or anything, Andrea, but my dad is a plastic surgeon. I was just wondering if you'd ever considered having some work done on your nose?'

Both of Andrea's hands came up over her face.

'What are you talking about?' she said. 'What's wrong with my nose?'

'You don't *know*?' Andy said innocently. 'Oh, wow, do I ever feel like a complete idiot. I'm really sorry, Andrea. There's absolutely nothing wrong with your nose. Pretend I never mentioned it. I'm really, really sorry.'

'*What's wrong with my NOSE*?' Andrea almost shrieked.

'Nothing, *honestly*,' Andy said. 'My dad always says, if people are happy with the way they look, then that's just fine.'

Andrea gave Andy such a *look*! Then she just turned and stormed off without saying another word.

'She's heading for the bathroom to take a look at her nose,' Fern giggled. 'That was brilliant, Andy!'

'I thought Stacy needed *out* of that conversation,' Andy said.

'Too right!' I said.

Pippa nodded wisely. 'She's suspicious of us.'

'Of course she is,' I said. 'Who wouldn't be? Wait until I see that big dumb sister of mine!'

Someone came whizzing up behind me and hissed in my ear.

'What did *she* want?'

I looked around. Amanda was crouching on the floor, staring over the table-top in Andrea's direction.

'She wanted to know what Mom and Dad do for a living,' I said.

Amanda let out a groan and hid her face in her hands.

'Oh, no!' she moaned. 'What did you tell her?'

I explained what I'd told Andrea.

'Stacy, you're wonderful!' Amanda squealed, giving me a big hug and kissing my forehead. 'Ew! Yuck! Sun oil! *Ptooie*!'

'She's really suspicious about us,' I said. 'I think we should stop this right now, before she comes up with some way of proving we're faking it.'

'Aw, not yet,' Andy said. 'I'm having fun. Anyway, I wanna tell her about my growing up on a nuclear submarine.'

'Yeah,' Fern added. 'And what about that time my math homework was stolen by aliens?'

Amanda looked thoughtful. Well, as thoughtful as a total airhead *can* look when she's crouching on the floor with her nose at table-level.

'No, Stacy's got a point,' she said after she'd finished thinking. 'It's a total waste of time trying to compete with Andrea. What we've got to do is finish her off once and for all.' Amanda's eyes gleamed. 'And I know just how to do it!'

Uh-oh. I didn't like the sound of that *at all*!

Chapter Ten

'I can't do it!' Pippa squealed.

'Sure, you can,' I said. 'When I count to three – jump!'

'OK.'

'One. Two. Three! *Go*!!!'

Neither of us moved.

'Pippa!' We were standing at the top of the water slide. Right on the brink. One step forward and we'd follow Fern and Andy down that long steep, winding, twisty, bumpy, slithery, bouncy slide to the pool thirty feet below us.

'Look!' I said, pointing down. 'There goes Fern.'

There was a big flume of white water as Fern cannonballed into the pool. There were plenty of other people in the water, splashing around and yelling and having a really good time.

It was the following day. Fern, Pippa, Andy

and I had all opted out of doing any of the organized stuff so that we could spend the morning in the pool.

After breakfast I had called home to tell Mom about the Open Day and to find out if she could come down and visit us. She'd said she wasn't sure, and that I'd have to get back to her.

Then we'd all made a bee-line for the pool. We changed into swimsuits, climbed the stairway up to the very top of the slide, and stared down at that long, long drop to the water.

And that was where Pippa had stalled. We tried coaxing her. Fern tried threatening her. Andy told her that *most* people reach the pool without breaking *every* bone in their body, which wasn't exactly helpful. But Pippa just stood there, hanging on to the rail with her eyes screwed tight shut and wouldn't jump.

'I'll go without you!' I told her sternly.

'OK. Fine.'

'You'll love it,' I said cheerily. Someone ran past us and went *wheeeeeeee* down the slide.

'I'm going back down,' Pippa said.

'OK, OK, you win,' I said. 'Take my hand and I'll lead you back.'

She took my hand. It was like being grabbed by a giant crab. Pippa sure was panicky. She hadn't even dared to open her eyes since we'd reached the platform. I led her away from the edge of the slide. Then I hauled her forwards without giving her time to brace herself.

'Stacee-ee-ee-ee-ee-ee!' she shrieked as the two of us went zooming down the slide.

It was fabulous! Half the time I didn't know which way was up. The slide snaked down, throwing us from side to side as we went faster and faster.

Then there were the bumps.

'*Yeeeow-urg! Yeeeow-urg*!' Pippa howled as we flew and bounced. '*Yeee-owww-wahhh*!'

SPLASH!!!!!

We hit the pool like a couple of rocks out of a catapult.

I swam to the side and wiped the water out of my eyes.

Pippa's head bobbed up right in front of me.

'I had to do it!' I spluttered.

'I wanna go again!' Pippa gasped. 'That was the most incredible thing *ever*!'

'Don't call me Stacy,' I reminded her. 'Yell, "La-a-a-aine" if you have to yell anything.'

'Oh. Yeah. Sorry.'

We climbed out of the pool. Fern and Andy were already halfway back up the stairs.

It was really strange how well those two got on. I mean, when Andy had first turned up at our favourite table in the school cafeteria back home, Fern had been really hostile to the idea of a *boy* hanging around with us. But now they got on really well.

There was a whole bunch of people lying on the grass all around the pool, or sprawled out on lounge chairs and towels, soaking up the sun. Pippa and I picked our way through them and headed back to the slide.

I spotted Andrea lying with another girl.

Andrea sat up. 'Hi, there,' she said, her eyes hidden by mirrored sunglasses. I was really surprised that she even spoke to us after the nose gag last night.

'Hi, Andrea,' I said. 'Aren't you going to do any swimming? I thought really good swimmers needed to practise every day.'

'I've been told not to,' Andrea came back at me, smooth as anything. 'I have a slight strain in my *gluteus maximus*, and my trainer said it needs total rest for a few weeks.'

'I see,' I said. 'Well, we're going on the slide again.'

Pippa and I walked past Andrea.

'Bye, *Stacy*,' she called.

I looked around with a smile. 'I'm Laine,' I said.

'Yeah, sorry,' Andrea smiled back. 'My mistake.'

Sure it was a mistake!

'Why did she call you Stacy?' Pippa asked as we climbed the steps of the slide.

'Beats me,' I said. 'Do you think she knows something?'

'Maybe she doesn't actually *know* anything,' Pippa said. 'But she sure is suspicious. Maybe Amanda or Rachel or someone said something to make her suspicious. You know how dumb Rachel can be. Anyway, my mom says that liars always suspect other people of lying. You know? Because they tell lies themselves.'

Yeah, maybe. And maybe Andrea had found something out. One thing was for sure. I was going to have to be real careful around that girl.

'Did you hear what she said about having a strain in her *gluttonous maximum*?' I said to Pippa. 'What the heck is a *gluttonous maximum*?'

'*Gluteus maximus*,' Pippa said. 'It's the big muscle in your rear end. She meant she has a pain in the butt.'

'Correction,' I said. 'She *is* a pain in the butt!'

* * *

I guess you might be wondering about Amanda's scheme for fixing Andrea. It involved Andrea's friend, Mary-Beth Kapowski. She was the girl Andrea was sunbathing with.

Andrea and Mary-Beth had come to camp together. When Andrea wanted to have any of her stories backed up, it was Mary-Beth who did the backing up. Mary-Beth was kind of unpleasant-looking, with short straight dark hair and a face that made me think of cartoon pigs. She had a really *snouty* kind of face, and mean little piggy eyes.

It's strange how girls who think they're totally and utterly gorgeous seem to hang out with real homely-looking friends. There's a girl back at our school called Judy MacWilliams, and her best pal, Maddie, looks like a warthog. I guess the ugly sidekicks make them think they look even more gorgeous.

Anyway, Amanda's plan was to sneak up on the two of them while they were on their own, and to listen to what they said to each other. Amanda figured that if they didn't realize they were being overheard, they might give something away.

ANDREA AND MARY-BETH GIVE SOMETHING AWAY
(From an idea by Fern Kipsak)

Andrea: Ah, now we are alone at last, agent Fphgrnnk, we can finally remove these hideous disguises.

Mary-Beth: Yes, agent Hrrrhrrugh. These stupid earthlings suspect nothing. Harr, harr!

Andrea: Ah, little do they know that our mothership lies hidden in orbit, waiting to unleash a reign of deadly terror down on this puny planet.

Mary-Beth: And once we have wiped out the humans, we will be able to set the great plan in motion. Earth will from thenceforth be known as Camp Nerkflonger, the greatest leisure complex ever created by the mighty Whoopthung race of the distant planet Poot.

(Fern's story went into a whole lot more detail than that, but you get the idea!)

What the rest of us *normal* people thought was that when Andrea and Mary-Beth were alone together, they might talk about where they really lived. They might even talk about how they were making complete monkeys out of *us*.

'And we can record them talking,' Amanda had said, 'using Stacy's new tape recorder.' I'd gotten the little battery-operated tape recorder for my birthday. I used it mostly to record messages for Cindy in San Diego. I'd brought it to camp with me so I could give Cindy a real feel for my vacation.

But Amanda was right. If we could sneak up on Andrea and Mary-Beth and actually record them blurting out about what their lives were *really* like, we'd have some hard evidence that would shut Andrea up for good!

'And once we've unmasked Andrea,' I had pointed out, 'we can tell her the truth about us! It won't matter then, because we'd have proved she was only telling stories, too!'

Amanda had looked at me. 'Uh, yeah, I guess so,' she'd said in the least-convincing voice I'd ever heard.

The thing was, that if Andrea had gotten suspicious about *us*, then we'd have to move pretty darned quickly, or *she* might unmask us before we got the chance to unmask her.

* * *

I met up with Amanda and the Bimbos at lunch time. They were sitting around one of the wooden picnic tables outside the Chuckwagon.

I shoved in between Amanda and Cheryl.

'I've got to talk to you,' I said. 'Andrea suspects something about me.'

'Uh-oh!' Cheryl said. 'What have you *done*?'

'I haven't done anything,' I said. I told them about what had happened earlier, when Andrea had called me Stacy to see how I'd react.

'And how *did* you react?' Natalie asked.

'I told her my name was Laine,' I said. 'How dumb do you think I am?'

'Do you want us to vote on that?' Cheryl asked.

'Cheryl, shut up!' Amanda said. 'This is serious.'

'No way is it serious,' Rachel said. 'Andrea's just *guessing*.'

'Yeah, maybe,' I said. 'But how come she's guessed *right*, huh?' I looked at Rachel. 'Maybe *you* said something.'

Rachel looked totally shocked. 'Me?' she squealed. 'Why me?'

'Did you say anything?' Amanda asked her.

'Rachel has already called me Stacy twice,' I said.

'I have only called you Stacy *once*, thank you very much,' Rachel said loudly.

'Shh!' Amanda hissed. The other picnic tables were full of people, but luckily Andrea and Mary-Beth weren't around. Not that Rachel had known that!

'See what I mean?' I said.

'Yeah, I see what you mean,' Amanda said. She looked at Rachel. 'Have you told *anyone* that Stacy is really *Stacy*?'

'No, of course not,' Rachel said. 'No one here, anyway.'

'What does that mean?' Cheryl asked.

'I might have mentioned it in the letter I wrote to Yvonne.' Yvonne was a cousin of Rachel's back in Four Corners. 'But that's all.'

'And you're sure there's no way Andrea could have seen the letter before you sent it?' I asked.

'What is this, *nerd*?' Rachel said to me, getting angry. 'The th-nerd degree?'

'Well?' Amanda asked. 'Could Andrea have seen the letter?'

'No way in the world,' Rachel said. 'Because, I remember now. I was in the cabin, and Andrea was outside. That's right. Andrea was walking past when she suddenly went, "Oh, my gosh, I've lost a contact lens!" And she asked me if I'd help her look for it. So I went out there. And Andrea was with me the whole time. Then I went back inside, finished the letter and put it straight in an envelope.' Rachel gave us a triumphant look. 'So, there. She couldn't have seen it.'

'Did you find the lens?' I asked.

'Huh?'

'Did you find Andrea's contact lens?' I asked really slowly so even Rachel would understand.

'No,' Rachel said. 'But she said it wasn't important, because they were disposable ones anyway.'

'And where was Mary-Beth while you were scratching around in the dirt looking for Andrea's contact lens?' I asked.

'How the heck should I know?' Rachel said.

'Oh, no!' Amanda groaned.

'It was a set up!' Cheryl said.

'And you fell for it, Rachel,' Natalie said.

'What are you guys talking about?' Rachel said.

'Andrea only pretended to lose her lens,' Amanda said. 'So you'd go out and help her look for it while Mary-Beth sneaked in behind you and read your letter.'

Rachel sat there with her mouth hanging open.

'You great dumb idiot!' Amanda said. 'So now she knows all about it!'

'No! Wait!' Rachel gabbled. 'I didn't write that Stacy was pretending to be Laine. That wasn't what I put. I just said something like it was really funny about all this Stacy and Laine stuff, and that I'd explain it all when I got home.' Rachel looked hopefully around at us. 'See? All I said was that it was funny. I didn't say *what* was funny.'

'OK,' Amanda said. 'So they don't know *exactly* what the deal is, but they know there's something phoney going on.'

'I think we should just confess the whole thing,' I said. 'I'd rather own up to it than be found out.'

'Who says we're going to be found out?' Amanda said.

'Amanda!' I said. 'Get real!'

She held her hand up. 'All this means,' she said, 'is that we've got to put Operation Eavesdrop forward to tonight.'

'Now wait a minute,' I started saying.

'We find out the truth about Andrea *tonight*,

guys,' Amanda said. 'And tomorrow we let her know that *we* know what a lying toad she is!'

I looked at Amanda. 'You mean, before she gets the chance to prove what a bunch of lying toads *we* are?' I said.

'Exactly!' Amanda said.

Chapter Eleven

'We've got to work together on this,' Amanda said. She looked at me. 'And that includes your friends as well.'

'We don't need *them*,' Cheryl said. 'They'll just mess up.'

'Fine with me,' I said, getting up. 'See you guys later.'

Amanda grabbed me and pulled me down again. She glared at Cheryl.

'Yes, we *do* need Stacy's friends,' she said.

'Laine's friends,' Rachel reminded her.

'Shut up!' Amanda said. 'The point is, if I can get a word in, that it's going to take all of us to keep watch on Andrea and Mary-Beth the whole time.'

'We can't just follow them around,' I said. 'They're going to notice. Especially if it's all *eight* of us!'

'It doesn't need to be all eight of us,' Amanda said. 'We've got to work something out.' She looked around the table. 'Stacy and – heck! *Laine* and I are going to have a summit meeting,' she said. 'You know, like presidents and prime minister-guys have when they need to discuss really important stuff.'

'So, what do we do while you and *her* are having your meeting?' Cheryl asked.

'You could go look for Andrea,' Amanda said. 'But don't let her see you, right?'

The Bimbos wandered off and Amanda and I got into a huddle at the table.

'First things first,' Amanda said. 'I'm in charge, OK?'

'Says who?' I asked.

'Says *me*,' Amanda said. 'And I'll sit on your head if you start arguing, got it?'

That sounded like a pretty compelling reason. Besides which, I was kind of intrigued to find out what ideas Amanda had thought up.

'OK, Big Chief,' I said. 'What's the plan?'

'Oh, uh, well,' Amanda said. 'I kind of hoped you'd come up with something.'

What did I call her before? Big Chief Air in the Head!

'OK,' I said, 'we can't all follow them at once, right?'

'Check!'

'So we need to draw up teams. Teams of, say, two people at a time. Like in a relay race. One team follows them for half an hour, and then they hand the tape recorder over to the next team, and so on.' I looked at Amanda to check that she was following me. 'And we just keep that up until we get the goods.'

Amanda nodded. 'Yeah,' she said. 'That's exactly what I was going to say. How do we pick teams?'

'We can put everyone's name in a bag and pull them out two at a time,' I said.

'Fine, and – oh, heck! It's *them*.'

I looked over my shoulder. Andrea and Mary-Beth were heading towards our table.

'Play it cool,' I whispered. 'Maybe they'll go past.' But it looked like the gruesome twosome were making straight for us. I couldn't see what Amanda was doing right then, so when she started speaking, I could hardly believe my ears!

'Hi, Stacy,' Amanda said, 'nice to hear from you. How's things?' I thought she'd lost her mind! I twisted my head around to look at her. *Now* I couldn't believe my *eyes*.

Amanda was speaking into a mobile phone. She must have whipped it out of her bag while I was looking over my shoulder. I didn't even know Amanda *had* a mobile phone. She sure didn't have one when she left home!

'How's the taping going, Stacy?' Amanda asked the mobile phone. 'It is? Great!' She smiled at me. 'Stacy says the taping is going just fine.'

'Oh, that's . . . uh . . . good,' I said.

'Hi, guys,' Andrea and Mary-Beth chorused in a way that sounded like they really meant '*Drop dead, guys.*'

'Hi,' Amanda said, with her hand over the end of the phone. 'I'm just talking to Stacy. She's taking a break between scenes.'

'Tell her I'm looking forward to watching the show,' Andrea said. 'When is it coming on?'

I saw Andrea and Mary-Beth exchange a sly look. Yeah, they were definitely suspicious.

'Hey, Stacy,' Amanda asked the phone, 'there are some guys here who'd like to know when the show will be on. Uh-huh? Oh. Right.' She looked up at Andrea. 'Sometime in the fall.'

'What channel will it be on?' Mary-Beth asked.

Amanda asked the phone.

'Stacy isn't sure,' Amanda said.

'You mean she doesn't know who she's

working for?' Andrea asked. 'Isn't that kind of *strange*?'

'Well, she, I, uh—'

I interrupted Amanda. 'The shows are being made by an independent company called N.R.G.,' I said. 'Then *they're* going to sell the series to the highest bidder.'

Phew! This was getting tricky.

'So the shows haven't actually been bought by a TV channel yet?' Andrea said.

'Stacy?' Amanda asked. 'We were just wondering – oh! Oh, right. Yeah. I understand. OK. I'll speak to you soon.' Amanda put the phone back in her bag and gave a shrug. 'She had to get back on set,' she said. 'They're taping a show with Ashley Mercury as the guest star and he's just arrived.' She smiled up at the two girls. 'You can't keep a star like Ashley Mercury waiting,' she said.

Amanda's imagination was back up in orbit! Not only were we supposed to attend the same school as Ashley Mercury, but *now* Amanda had him guest-starring in *Stacy, Stacy*!

'N.R.D. must be, like, super-rich if they can afford to hire Ashley Mercury,' Andrea said. 'I'm totally amazed that I've never heard of them.'

'N.R.G.,' I corrected her. 'They're new kids

on the block in Hollywood,' I explained. 'They're financed by a billionaire oil tycoon from Texas. Archibald Q Bippy the Third.'

'Hey, Laine,' Amanda said, 'we'd better go and get your sunblock from your cabin before you fry.'

I took the hint. I wanted out of that situation as much as Amanda did. Another couple of tricky questions from Andrea and we'd be in trouble.

'Catch you later,' Amanda called as we headed to the cabins. 'Have a nice day.'

'Ashley Mercury?' I said once we were well out of earshot. 'Are you kidding?'

'Well, what about you?' Amanda said. 'Archibald Q Bippy the Third? What kind of a name is that?'

'What do you expect?' I snapped. 'I was making stuff up as I went along! And I didn't notice you helping out! You were just sitting there with your *brain* running out of your ears! And where the heck did you get that mobile phone from?'

'It's Cheryl's,' Amanda said. 'Well, it's her dad's really, but she kind of borrowed it from him. She's letting me use it to pretend I'm talking to Stacy in Hollywood when Andrea is hanging around.' Amanda took the phone out of her shoulder bag.

'Hi,' she said into it, 'this is Amanda speaking. I'd like to have Andrea Wolfson encased in cement and dumped at sea, please. Uh-huh? Fine! Send the bill to my sister Stacy, care of Beverly Hills.' Amanda grinned at me. 'Don't you think I look totally sophisticated and grown-up with this, huh?'

'I think it looks like a mobile phone with an *airhead* attachment,' I said. 'Sheesh, Amanda! You're get getting us deeper and deeper into trouble every time you open your mouth. I mean, Ashley Mercury! Andrea is *never* going to believe that.'

'It doesn't matter *what* Andrea believes,' Amanda said with a toss of her hair. 'Once we've got the goods on *her*, she won't be able to show her *face* around here! And we're going to get her but good, Stacy.'

Yeah, we *hope*!

* * *

'No way am I teaming up with Rachel,' Fern said. 'Andy can have Rachel. I'll take Cheryl.'

Amanda and I had finished our summit meeting in her cabin and we'd picked out the teams for *Operation Eavesdrop*. The draw had worked so that I was with Amanda. Pippa was with Natalie. Andy was with Cheryl and Fern had the booby prize.

Now all I had to do was sell the idea to my friends. I'd gotten them all together in Wampum cabin and I'd explained the plan to them. Fern didn't take it too well.

'It was all totally fair,' I said. 'We picked the names out of a bag. You were just unlucky.' I gave Fern a hopeful smile. 'It won't be so awful, honest. Rachel's not *that* bad.'

'She is that bad,' Fern insisted. 'And how come you and Amanda got to team up together, huh?'

'Did your names go in the bag?' Andy asked.

'Not exactly,' I had to admit.

'Hah!' Fern exclaimed. 'You total cheat! Well, that fixes it! No way am I teaming up with Rachel.' She pointed at me. '*You* get Rachel. I'll take Amanda.'

'But—'

'Hey, don't worry, *Laine*,' Fern said. 'After all, Rachel's not *that* bad.'

And from the determined look on Fern's face, it didn't seem like I had a whole lot of choice.

Chapter Twelve

Operation Eavesdrop

Amanda and I had decided that each team should keep tabs on Andrea and Mary-Beth for an hour before handing over to the next team. We'd tossed a dime to pick what order the teams watched in. Rachel and I had gotten fourth shift.

I was really pleased about that, because it meant I had most of the afternoon to do other things. And the first other thing I did was to call home.

I told Mom all about the camp. 'There are counsellors to teach sports stuff and wildlife stuff,' I told her. 'And I learned how to roll a kayak right over. And the slide into the pool is completely amazing, although it took us forever to get Pippa down it.'

'And are you getting along OK with Amanda?'

'We're getting along fine,' I said. 'Amanda's

just about taken over the camp cheerleading squad, and they're working on a special routine for Open Day tomorrow. Mom, are you going to be able to make it?'

'Oh, honey, I'm sorry,' Mom said. 'It's just not possible. I'd love to, but I'm really snowed under. And your dad is away for three whole days.'

'Oh, OK,' I said, trying not to sound too disappointed.

'But you might get a nice surprise,' Mom said mysteriously. '*Someone* might be there.'

'Who?'

'Just wait and see.'

Mom likes to tease a little sometimes, and I could tell from her voice that she wasn't going to let me know who might be coming to visit the camp for the Open Day.

'How's Benjamin?' I asked.

Mom laughed. 'I wondered how long it would take you to ask that,' she said. 'He's fine. Last I saw, he was asleep in the laundry basket.'

After I called Mom, I met up with Pippa and we headed over to the camp office to sign up for rock climbing later in the week. Pippa and Natalie's team were on number three Andrea-watch, right before Rachel and me.

'If you ask me,' Pippa said, 'this whole thing is a total waste of time. If we want to find out the truth about Andrea, we're going to have to be a whole lot more cunning than just following her around.' She gave me a sneaky look. 'We're going to have to out-think her, see? We're going to have to use our *brains*.' She tapped the side of her head. 'I've been doing some thinking,' she said, nodding slowly.

I tried to forget all about the Pippa-jinx. Maybe this *once* she'd come up with a good plan.

'Uh-huh?' I said dubiously. 'And?'

'It's simple,' Pippa said. 'We kind of casually ask her the name of the hotel in New York where her folks live, and then we call the hotel and ask them whether the Wolfson family have a floor there or not.'

I tried to come up with some reason why Pippa's plan wouldn't work. I mean, it *sounded* really good. But then *all* Pippa's plans *sound* good. It's not until a person actually tries them that you find out all the things that can go wrong. And, believe me, Pippa has a real knack for coming up with schemes that go totally haywire.

'Anyway,' Pippa said. 'I'm going to try it.

The way I see it, I could have this case solved in ten seconds flat.' She stopped to think. 'Well, half an hour, anyway.'

* * *

Fern and Amanda had first watch in *Operation Eavesdrop*. By the look of it, Andrea and Mary-Beth were planning on spending most of the afternoon sunbathing down by the lake.

Apparently Fern and Amanda had started arguing almost immediately. Amanda looked half-crazy when I met up with her an hour later.

'That girl is totally nuts,' Amanda said. 'She kept trying to tell me how Mary-Beth was really a robot and that Andrea was working her by remote control. I mean, come on! Earth to Fern!'

Yeah, that sounded like Fern.

Just then Fern came trotting over. Amanda took one look at her and walked real quickly in the opposite direction.

'You know the problem with your sister?' Fern said. 'She can't handle new ideas.'

Fern and I got ourselves involved in a game of softball. I'm not usually very good at stuff like that, but by some total *fluke* I hit a home run. It was kind of annoying that Amanda wasn't there to see it! She was always teasing me about being as sporty as a cabbage.

Later in the afternoon I went over to the lake. Andrea and Mary-Beth hadn't moved. Pippa and Natalie were sitting several yards apart, facing in different directions and looking totally annoyed with each other.

'What's wrong?' I asked Pippa. They were about twenty yards away from Andrea and Mary-Beth, so there wasn't any problem with being overheard.

'We were only supposed to *watch*!' Natalie said. 'But your bozo friend had to go over and start asking them *questions*.'

'*A* question,' Pippa insisted. 'One single question. All I asked was the name of the hotel Andrea lived in. What's so terrible about that?'

'What did she say?' I asked Pippa.

'She said her parents don't like her telling people the name,' Pippa said, 'because they don't want to have to fight through a load of photographers and reporters every time they leave home.'

Yeah, that sounded like the kind of thing Andrea would say. I glanced over to where the two of them were lying. Andrea was on her stomach, reading a magazine. As I looked over there, she lowered her sunglasses and stared straight at me.

I pretended I wasn't really looking at her at all, but I was sure she *knew* what we were up to.

And she knew that we *knew* that she knew what we were up to. And she didn't care that we knew that she knew that we knew that . . . well, you get the picture!

'This,' I said slowly, 'is a total waste of time. We're about as likely to overhear Andrea saying anything incriminating as Rachel is to win the Young Brain of America competition.'

'What was that about me?' Rachel came strolling over in the world's most stupid sombrero and a pair of sunglasses with lime-green, fluorescent frames. They matched her green swimsuit. She looked like a radioactive stick insect.

'They were just trying to be funny,' Natalie said, glaring at us. 'And *failing*.'

'Give me the tape recorder,' Rachel said.

'OK,' Natalie took the recorder out of her shoulder bag and handed it over to Rachel. 'I hope you have better luck than we did.'

'Luck just isn't going to come into it,' Rachel said.

'For heaven's sake!' I said. 'Could you guys

try to be a little more *obvious*? I think there's someone over on the far side of the *state* who hasn't figured what we're doing.'

'Chill out,' Rachel said to me. 'Everything's just fine.' She looked around. 'OK. Where do we sit, huh?' She pointed over towards Andrea and Mary-Beth.

'Hey,' she said loudly. 'That looks like a good place.' She marched right over, spread her towel on the grass and plonked herself down about a yard and a half away from Andrea.

'I'm going to have to kill her,' I murmured as I headed over to where she was sitting. She was almost totally shaded by her sombrero, but she was smearing sun oil on herself as thick as peanut butter.

I sat down so she was between me and Andrea.

'Pretend we're not talking about anything much,' Rachel whispered. 'I'll put the recorder here, OK?' She sat it between us on her towel. 'If they start talking, I'll switch it on, got it?'

'Got it,' I sighed. I mean, like they'd start blurting out their darkest secrets with the two of us lying four feet away!

I covered all my exposed skin with sunblock and lay down in the grass. Well, I might as well make myself comfortable while *nothing* happened!

* * *

I woke up with Rachel poking me in the ribs.

'Quit that, Amanda!' I said. I opened an eye and saw Rachel and her sombrero staring down at me. 'Oh, it's *you*.'

'They've gone,' Rachel said. She waved the tape recorder under my nose. 'I've got some stuff on here. I tricked them into thinking I'd fallen asleep.'

I sat up. The sun was lower down in the sky across the other side of the lake. I must have been asleep for some time.

'I made out I was snoring, see?' Rachel explained. 'And you're not going to believe what they said. It's all true! Honest to gosh! Everything she's said about herself is totally true!'

'Let me listen to that,' I said.

I took the tape player from Rachel and rewound the tape to the beginning. Then I pressed play.

'She started off by saying it was a shame her folks couldn't come to the Open Day,' Rachel said. 'That's when I sneakily turned the tape on. Listen.'

I could hardly hear a word Andrea was saying over the snoring noises that Rachel was making.

'That's me pretending to be asleep,' Rachel said.

'No kidding?' I said.

I rewound the tape and listened again. This time, by concentrating really hard I could just make out what Andrea was saying.

'. . . and Mommy was really looking forward to visiting tomorrow. It's, like, a total drag that she's got to fly over to Italy for that exclusive clothes show.' Andrea let out a big sigh. 'It's not always easy being the only child of an internationally famous clothes designer and perfumier. I mean, it's not like I'm complaining or anything, and I know I'll inherit all those millions of dollars and stuff one day, but I'd really like for my folks to have a little time for me now and then.'

I heard a giggle in the background.

'Shhh!' Andrea hissed.

'Sorry,' Mary-Beth whispered.

'Anyway,' Andrea said in an unnaturally loud voice. 'Daddy is, like, totally busy in China, negotiating that huge trade deal, so I guess I won't be having any visitors at all tomorrow. It's a real downer, but what's a person to do, huh?' There was a pause and then Andrea said, 'I think I'll go call Mommy one last time before she leaves home. I can ask her if she's ever heard of a Texas oil billionaire called Archibald Q Bippy.' The voice faded. I guessed Andrea had stood up. 'I'm sure Mommy *will* have heard of him,' she said, 'because if Mommy hasn't heard of a person, then I guess that person just doesn't *exist*.'

I listened for a few more seconds, but all I could hear was Rachel's fake snoring. I pressed the stop button.

'You see?' Rachel said. 'It must all be true! But who the heck is that billionaire guy she was talking about?'

'I think we need to find Amanda,' I said. 'Like, now.'

* * *

We were in Amanda's cabin. There was no one else in there except for Cheryl, Amanda, Rachel and me. We were sitting on Cheryl's top bunk bed, listening to the tape again.

'They're faking it,' Cheryl said.

'No way,' Rachel butted in. 'Why should they do that? They thought I was asleep. They didn't know anyone was listening. Why would

Andrea say all that stuff with no one listening? It's all true, I tell you.'

'So why did Mary-Beth start laughing?' Amanda asked. 'And that's the least convincing snoring I've ever heard, Rachel.'

'Face it, guys,' I said, '*Operation Eavesdrop* just isn't going to work. She's too smart for you.'

'For *us*, you mean,' Cheryl said.

'Hmmmm,' I said. 'If you say so.'

I climbed down off the bed.

'Oh, well,' I said, 'see you around, guys.' I left them looking really gloomy up on Cheryl's bed.

I saw Natalie outside the cabin.

'If you're looking for the three dumb monkeys,' I said as I walked past her. 'They're in *there*.'

'Say what?'

'The three dumb monkeys,' I called back with a grin. 'Do nothing smart, say nothing smart and think nothing smart.'

'Ver-ry funny,' Natalie said. 'Hey, and when you see Pippa, tell her no way am I teaming up with her again!'

* * *

I found the gang and we went for a snack and a milk shake in the Chuckwagon.

'So,' I said. '*Operation Eavesdrop* was a total washout. What do we do now?'

'There's no way that I'm doing *anything* ever again,' Andy said firmly, 'that involves having to spend time with Cheryl. She's bossy and sarcastic and stupid and big-headed.'

Pippa nodded. 'That sounds exactly like Natalie.'

'And Amanda,' Fern added.

'Huh!' I said. 'You guys had it easy. I had to put up with Rachel.' I took a slurp of chocolate shake. 'Let's face it,' I said, 'if we want to outsmart *anyone*, the first thing we need to do is dump the Bimbos. Agreed?'

They all agreed.

'And between the four of us,' I continued, 'I'm betting we can come up with something really cunning and sneaky and brilliant.' I grinned. 'In fact, I already have a plan. All we need is a volunteer. Someone fearless and super-smart.'

'I vote for Andy,' Fern said quickly.

'Seconded!' Pippa gabbled before Andy had the chance to even open his mouth.

'Hey, wait a minute,' Andy began.

'All in favour,' I said. Pippa, Fern and I put our hands up. 'All opposed?'

Andy's hand went up like a rocket.

'Three to one,' I said. 'Andy's our man.'

Andy put his head in his hands and made moaning noises.

'Hey, don't worry about it,' I said, patting him reassuringly on the back. 'It's going to be really easy. Honest it is.'

Chapter Thirteen

To be honest, it was Andrea herself who had given me the idea. Remember how she'd tricked Rachel into helping her look for a contact lens while Mary-Beth snuck into the cabin and nosed through Rachel's things?

Well, if that kind of behaviour was OK for Andrea, then it was sure OK for *us*. I mean, I wouldn't *normally* stoop to that kind of thing, but, hey, Andrea's a special case, right? And she started it!

And now that we'd lost the Bimbos, I reckoned we'd be able to finish it.

My plan was fiendish in its simplicity. (I love that line! I got it from a book.)

Stacy's Fiendishly Simple Ten Point Plan

1. Pippa waits in the Chuckwagon at dinner time.

2. Andrea and Mary-Beth arrive for dinner.
3. Pippa signals to me. I am waiting outside the Chuckwagon.
4. I signal to Fern, who is waiting halfway between the Chuckwagon and Andrea's cabin.
5. Fern signals to Andy, who is waiting by Andrea's cabin.
6. Andy sneaks in and finds something to prove that Andrea is the biggest storyteller in the entire universe.
7. We confront Andrea.
8. Andrea admits everything.
9. Andrea is defeated, so we tell her the truth about us.
10. Everyone makes friends.

We sat at a picnic table near the lake while I explained my plan to the others.

'But what am I supposed to be looking for?' Andy was still asking ten minutes before dinner time.

'How should I know?' I said. 'Something to prove Andrea doesn't have a millionaire *mommy* or a mega-important *daddy*, or something to prove she doesn't live on an entire floor of a New York hotel.'

'Use your initiative, Andy,' Pippa said. 'Look for something with a home address on it. Anything to prove she's just ordinary like us.'

'We're not *ordinary,*' Fern said. 'We come from Beverly Hills.'

I looked at her. 'We've got to act quickly, guys,' I said. 'Fern's starting to *believe* it!'

Just then the Native-American drums came thundering out over the PA system. That always meant there was about to be an announcement.

'It's camp fire night at Camp Powhatan!' called a cheerful voice. 'Toasted marshmallows and a singalong, just like the olden days.' In the background, behind the voice, one of those *yippee-aii-ayyy* type cowboy songs was being played. 'Come on, all you pioneers, and join in the fun at the south side of the lake tonight. Yee-hah!'

'Sounds great,' Andy said. 'What say we forget all about Andrea and—'

'Nice try, Andy,' I interrupted. 'But no deal.'

I looked at my watch.

It was zero hour minus five minutes.

'Time to go,' I said.

Andy looked at me. 'Have I ever told you I

hate it when you have ideas?' he said. 'I know what's going to happen. I'm going to get caught in that cabin, and I'm going to be torn to pieces by a bunch of crazy girls.'

'Don't worry about it,' Fern said. 'I'll be keeping watch. Believe me, *nothing* can go wrong!'

* * *

Something went wrong.

Everything started off just fine. Andrea and Mary-Beth went to the Chuckwagon. Pippa signalled to me. I signalled to Fern and half a minute later Fern did the thumbs-up sign back to me to show that Andy had gone into the cabin.

I looked in through the Chuckwagon window to signal to Pippa that everything was going according to plan. But Pippa wasn't there any more.

Pippa had disappeared.

I was just wondering what had happened to her, when she came running around the corner of the building and almost crashed straight into me.

'They've gone!' Pippa panted. 'They've both gone! I only turned my back for a second.

They must have sneaked out the back way. What do we do now?'

'Don't panic,' I said. 'Maybe they just went to the bathroom.'

'No. I checked.'

'OK,' I said. 'You go and warn Fern. If they turn up there, try and stall them until Andy can get out.'

'Stall them how?'

'Ask for their autographs,' I babbled, 'kick them in the shins, fake a heart attack! *Anything*! I'm going to try and find them.'

Pippa ran off.

I had to think quickly. If Andrea and Mary-Beth had been heading back to their own cabin, they'd have passed me. They hadn't passed me, which meant they were going somewhere else. But where?

I ran around the building. Maybe they were doing something totally innocent, like heading for the reception area to make a phone call?

I caught sight of the two of them around the back of the Chuckwagon. They weren't heading anywhere near the phones. They were walking quickly along the path that led to the baseball diamond and the tennis courts.

Suddenly they headed off the path and out

of sight behind Beaver cabin. They were definitely up to something sneaky.

I followed them. Yeah! I *knew* it! Just about everyone was in the Chuckwagon right then, which meant that people who wanted to sneak into another person's cabin could do it without being spotted. And that was exactly what Andrea and Mary-Beth were doing.

I saw them glance around and then dive in through the door of the cabin where Amanda and the others slept.

The nerve of those girls! I knew exactly what they were doing. They were in there hoping to find something to prove we'd been making it all up about Beverly Hills and our TV-star sister.

STACY'S CONSCIENCE: May I just point out that you sent Andy into Andrea's cabin to do the same thing?

STACY: I'd really prefer it if you *didn't* point that out right now.

STACY'S CONSCIENCE: OK. Forget I spoke.

Grr! I hate that conscience sometimes!

I snuck up to the cabin and slowly edged my eyes up over the windowsill. The window was open a little.

'How should I know where her stuff is?'

Andrea was saying. 'We'll have to search. Hey! Wait a second. Look, it's that dumb carrot-headed geek's stupid sombrero.'

I could see Andrea and Mary-Beth in the cabin. They ran over to one end, where Rachel's sombrero was lying on her bunk.

'OK,' Andrea said. 'Amanda's stuff will be around here somewhere.'

'We've gotta be quick,' Mary-Beth whimpered. 'What if we get caught?'

'We won't,' Andrea said. 'Those guys are the dumbest bunch of airheads I've ever met. Like, I'd never have guessed they were keeping watch on us all day!' I saw Andrea grin nastily. 'We left that goofy-looking kid staring at our empty seats in the cafeteria.' She laughed. 'Fooling them is almost *too* easy, you know? I mean, a person likes a challenge.'

The goofy-looking kid was obviously Pippa.

'I think I've found her stuff,' Mary-Beth said. I hardly dared breathe as I watched the two of them open the locker next to Amanda's bunk.

'Yeah, this is it,' Andrea said.

What should I do? Rush in there and make a citizen's arrest? I had the unpleasant feeling that Andrea and Mary-Beth wouldn't be too pleased at being disturbed. They might decide to use me as a football.

On the other hand, if I ran for help, the pair of them could be out of there before I got back.

'Darn,' Andrea said. 'There's nothing any good in here at all!'

She sat on Amanda's bed with a really ferocious scowl on her face.

'What do we do now?' Mary-Beth asked. 'Hey, we could make her an apple-pie bed!'

Andrea gave her a sour-lemon look. 'Mary-Beth,' she said, 'sometimes I totally give up! This isn't *kid's* stuff. I need some way of proving once and for all that Amanda and the whole stupid bunch of them are total liars!' Her eyes narrowed to evil little slits. 'And then I'm going to *humiliate* them in front of the whole camp!'

That was what I'd been afraid of right from the start.

Andrea gave a sudden whoop. 'Mary-Beth! I've got it!' she yelled. 'I'm so dumb! It's been staring me right in the face all along. I know *exactly* what to do!'

Uh-oh! That didn't sound too good.

'What are you going to do, Andrea?' Mary-Beth asked.

'I'm going to trick her into calling that so-called TV-star sister of hers on her mobile phone,' Andrea said. 'And then I'm going to force her to let me speak to her.'

'Oh.' Through the window slit I could see the blank look on Mary-Beth's face. 'How will that help?'

'You dummy!' Andrea said. 'It'll help because I'm certain she doesn't *have* a TV-star sister! Their whole story is a heap of garbage, and I'm betting there won't be *anyone* on the other end of the phone. She just calls a fake number and *pretends* to talk to someone.'

Oops! Good guess, Andrea.

'Andrea, that's brilliant!' Mary-Beth said.

'Yeah, it is, isn't it?' Andrea said smugly. 'Come one, let's get out of here. Let's go find Amanda!'

Oh, boy! I had to find Amanda before Andrea did. I had to *warn* her! But where *was* she? I hadn't seen Amanda or any of the Bimbos since I'd left them in their cabin earlier that afternoon.

The Chuckwagon!

I raced down the path as fast as I could. Amanda had to lose that mobile phone so that she couldn't be tricked into pretending to call Hollywood. She'd have to bury it or dump it in the lake or *eat* it or something! Just so long as it was gone before Andrea found her.

The Chuckwagon was as crowded as always at meal times. There was a counsellor on the PA, telling people that the camp fires had been lit over by the lake and that the marshmallows were waiting to be toasted on the end of sticks.

I climbed up on a chair so I could see better. But there wasn't a Bimbo in the place. Maybe they were already heading over to the lake.

Run, Stacy, run!

Andy, Pippa and Fern were on the path outside the Chuckwagon.

'Have you seen Amanda?' I panted.

'Not recently, why?' Pippa asked. 'What's wrong?'

'What's going on?' Andy asked before I had the chance to catch my breath. 'I'd only been in Andrea's cabin for ten seconds when Fern signalled me to get out of there. Where *is* Andrea?'

An idea suddenly hit me. A brilliant idea, if only I had enough time to set it up!

'I can't explain right now,' I panted. 'Look, it's really important that Amanda doesn't use her mobile phone, OK?'

'Why not?' Fern said.

'Trust me!' I yelled, already running back

the way I'd come. 'Find Amanda. Don't let her use the phone. I'll explain later!'

For my plan to work, I had to make an important phone call of my own. And I had to make it right *now.* And then I had to find Amanda before Andrea sprang her trap.

But for things to work out the way I hoped, I was going to have to move faster than I'd ever moved in my life!

Chapter Fourteen

I was pretty much exhausted by the time I'd made my call and then gotten all the way up to the lake. I had a really bad stitch in my side and I was panting for breath. Having brilliant ideas sure can wear a person out!

Four camp fires had been lit along the south side of the lake. The PA system was playing cowboy music and there were already plenty of people sitting around in groups talking and laughing and singing along to *'Home, home on the range, where the deer and the antelope play . . .'*

I ran past a bunch of people toasting marsh-mallows on the end of twigs. I didn't have time for stuff like that. I had to find Amanda.

I saw a commotion a little way off. It was *them*!

I ran up, but for a few seconds I was too breathless to speak.

'Give me that!' Pippa was saying. She was

struggling with Amanda. They each had hold of something and the two of them were fighting over it.

'Are you completely nuts?' Amanda shrieked. 'Let go my phone!'

'No!' Pippa gasped. 'You're not to use it!'

The other Bimbos were standing around looking baffled. Andy and Fern stood there looking like they wished they were some place else, and Andrea and Mary-Beth had the most smug looks on their faces that you could imagine.

I could guess what had happened. Andrea had already asked Amanda to call Stacy. Amanda had taken her phone out and Pippa, following my instructions, had *pounced* to stop her using it.

The only problem was that the whole idea had been to keep the mobile phone *hidden*, not to wrestle it out of Amanda's hands in front of Andrea and Mary-Beth.

Amanda gave a final wrench and Pippa lost grip of her end of the phone.

'Thank you!' Amanda said. 'You are some kind of monster cuckoo-brain, Pippa!'

'But Stacy said—' Pippa stopped dead.

'What did Stacy say?' Andrea asked slyly.

'Nothing,' Pippa said.

'Stacy said *nothing*?' Andrea said.

'That's right,' Pippa said with a sickly grin. 'I mean, she's in California. How could she have said anything? Well, she *could* have said something, but I wouldn't have been able to hear it. I'm way over *here* and she's way over . . . uh, *there*, so I couldn't have heard her say anything. Well, not unless I was some kind of *psychic* or something.'

'Pippa.' Fern said, 'you're babbling.'

Pippa went quiet.

'Crazy,' Amanda said, shaking her head sadly. 'I guess it must be the heat.' And then she started punching out her fake dialling code.

In case you were wondering what *I* was doing all this time, I was bent over with my hands on my knees, sucking in as much oxygen as I could and waiting for my heartbeat to drop below two hundred a minute!

'Oh, hi, Stacy?' Amanda said into the phone. 'How did the taping go? Uh-huh? Yeah? That's great, Stacy! I've got a friend over here who wants to know what it was like working with Ashley Mercury.'

That was the moment Andrea had been waiting for. She made a lunge for the phone.

'Let me speak to her,' Andrea said.

(In a movie, this would have been a really cool slow-motion scene.)

Amanda jerked back, looking totally surprised. Andrea swiped the phone clean out of her hand. But I took a flying leap and grabbed the phone out of Andrea's fingers before she could get a good grip on it.

'I want to talk to Stacy first!' I yelled as I flew through the air with the phone clutched in my hands.

'What's going on here?' Amanda yelled.

'It looks like everyone wants a piece of Stacy,' Andy said.

I put the phone to my ear. 'Hello? Stacy? Oh, heck, she's been cut off!'

Andrea glared at me. 'Oh, *sure*!' she said. 'Like, as if she was ever *there* in the first place!'

Amanda put her fists on her hips. 'And just exactly what is that crack supposed to mean?' she demanded.

'I'll tell you exactly what it means,' Andrea said. 'It means you don't *have* a TV-star sister! It means you're one big, dumb *fake*, Amanda. You and all your big, dumb fake friends!'

I dialled a number. 'Hey, guys,' I said, 'can you hold the noise down a little, please? I want to speak to Stacy.'

Andrea turned and glared at me. 'Liar!' she spat.

'OK, Andrea,' I said. '*You* talk to her.'

Andrea took the phone from me and held it to her ear.

'It's ringing,' she said blankly. 'What kind of a dumb trick is this? If you think for one second, that— oh! Oh! OH! Yeah, uh, I . . .' she said into the phone. 'Is this the right number for Stacy Allen?'

You should have seen Amanda's face right then. In fact, I wish I'd taken a picture of the whole bunch of them. They were all standing there looking like the sky was about to come crashing in on them.

'It *is*?' Andrea gasped. 'Stacy Allen the TV actor? Oh, cripes! I'm sorry! You sound younger than I'd expected. I didn't mean, I don't . . . uh, yeah. Sure. Yeah, I understand. No, no, *honestly*, I wouldn't do that. Your sister Laine gave me the phone. No, no, I don't have your private number. Listen, *honest to gosh*, I don't have your private number.' Andrea handed the phone back to me as if it was red hot.

'She thinks I've stolen her private number,' she gabbled. 'Tell her I *haven't*.'

I put the phone to my ear.

'Hi, it's Laine,' I said.

'Did it work?' said my mysterious voice. 'Did I do good?'

'Sure thing,' I said.

'Tell her I didn't steal her phone number!' Andrea almost shrieked.

'Hey, Stacy?' I said. 'That was a real good friend of ours, and she didn't steal your personal phone number, OK?'

I could hear giggling down the other end of the phone.

I pretended to be listening to Stacy telling me stuff for a few seconds, then I said, 'OK, I'll give your love to Amanda. 'Bye!'

I handed the phone back to a totally amazed-looking Amanda.

'Stacy sends her love,' I said.

'Oh, fine,' Amanda mumbled.

I looked at Andrea. 'Stacy says sorry she was a little cranky with you, but she's been working with Ashley Mercury all day, and he's such a total perfectionist that they've had to take some shots over and over before he was satisfied.' I looked at Amanda. 'And she said not to call her for a few days, because she's going to be snowed under with work.'

Amanda's not the most brilliant person in

the world, but even *she* had realized by then that I'd set something up.

She put the phone into her bag and gave us all a big smile.

'Who's for toasted marshmallows?' she said.

'Just a second,' I said, looking at Andrea. 'Were you saying something about being a big, dumb fake? And didn't I hear you use the word *liar* at some stage?'

'Yeah, well, I, no, but . . .' Andrea spluttered.

'I mean,' I said smoothly, 'if people were calling other people names, then what names would you use for people who sneaked into other people's cabins when they weren't there and snooped through their things, huh, Andrea?'

'What?' Amanda growled. 'Who's been sneaking into *whose* cabin and doing *what*?'

'Do you want to confess, Andrea?' I asked. 'Or should I just go tell one of the counsellors?'

Andrea's face went bright red. She made a few choking, gurgling noises and then just turned and ran off with Mary-Beth scampering along at her heels.

Everyone looked at me.

'What?' I said.

'What did you do?' Amanda gasped. 'Who was she *talking* to on the other end of the phone?'

'Oh, *that*,' I said. 'That was just Cindy. I called her up from the payphone a few minutes ago and told her to expect a call from someone who'd ask if she was Stacy Allen the TV star. I told her to say, yes, she was and to act really annoyed at being disturbed.' I grinned. 'Judging by Andrea's reaction, I think she did really well. What do you think, Amanda?'

Remember, I told you earlier that my best friend, Cindy Spiegel had moved to California? Well, if a person can't rely on her best friend to do her a big favour, then who can a person rely on?

Hey, hang out the flags! Call up the brass band! For maybe the first time in her entire life, my sister was totally, utterly and completely *speechless*!

Chapter Fifteen

I was woken up the next morning by something heavy landing on my chest.

'Benjamin!' I mumbled. 'Get out of here. It's too early.'

'Meow,' said a voice. Not a cat voice.

I opened one eye.

'Hello,' Amanda said, 'I've brought breakfast in bed for the smartest sister a person ever had.'

'I forgot where I was,' I said with a sleepy grin. I sat up and looked at the tray that Amanda had dumped on me.

'Breakfast?' I said. 'A can of Coke, a pack of gummi bears and two candy bars?'

'It was all I could find,' Amanda explained. 'The line in the Chuckwagon went on forever so I went to the store instead. Anyway, it's the thought that counts.'

'I guess so,' I said. I looked around. A few people in the cabin were still curled up in bed, but most were starting to get up and were running around in pyjamas or underwear, or scribbling cards home or talking together.

Fern was in the bunk above Pippa. She climbed out of the covers and gave a huge stretch.

She leaned right over the edge of her bed. 'Hey, Pippa!' she yelled. 'Wake up!'

'*Hurggruumph*,' Pippa muttered. 'Five minutes. I can't open my eyes yet.'

Fern jumped down and bounced on Pippa's bed.

'Fern!'

'Can you open your eyes now?' Fern giggled. 'Come on. We've got places to go and people to see. It's Open Day, there's the concert and the picnic and everything.'

'And the cheerleaders,' Amanda said. 'We've come up with a really good cheer.' She grinned at me. 'And the best part,' she said softly so that the other girls in the cabin wouldn't hear, 'is the fact that Andrea won't dare show her face anywhere *near* us after last night. We *won*!'

'Yeah, great,' I said. 'We won the *Liars of the Year* award. I'm really proud of *that*!'

'Oh, come on,' Amanda said in a quiet voice. 'That kind of thing's not real lying. It's just making stuff up for fun. We had to get even with Andrea somehow. Do you really believe she's been telling us the truth?'

'No, I guess not,' I said. 'But I think *we* should. Otherwise we're no better than her.' I looked carefully at Amanda. 'I think we should own up. We can say it was just a *game*.'

Amanda gazed at me with a thoughtful look in her eyes.

'Do you really want to do that?' she said.

I nodded.

'OK,' Amanda sighed. 'But can we leave it until tomorrow? Andrea's bound to make a big deal out of it. Let's at least get through Open Day without half the camp thinking we're total jerks.'

'It's a deal!' I said.

I felt kind of relieved that we'd finally agreed to come clean about Beverly Hills and *Stacy, Stacy* and Dynamo Duke Logan and Ashley Mercury and all that Hollywood stuff.

And once all *that* was dealt with, then maybe we could forget all about Andrea Wolfson and start having a really good time.

* * *

There was a whole lot of work being done to prepare the camp for Open Day. Counsellors were running around like crazy ants, putting up notices and posters and decorations. And one bunch was setting up the stage for the concert down by the lake. The PA was playing pop music interrupted by announcements telling people what to do and where to go and when the show was going to start.

Amanda and her friends had vanished somewhere to practise their cheerleading routine. Pippa, Andy, Fern and I were just wandering around checking things out and having fun. No one had seen Andrea all morning.

'Maybe she went home?' Andy suggested.

'I hope so,' I said. 'And I hope she's taken Mary-Beth with her.'

'I guess she's probably just hiding somewhere,' Fern said. 'I'd feel like hiding if I'd been caught out the way she was. I'd dig myself a hole and live in it for the rest of the summer.'

We found a bench in the middle of the camp and sat down to watch the first visitors' cars pull into the parking lot.

Some stalls had been set up over there. A couple of them had leaflets about the day's events and about the camp, and others sold Camp Powhatan T-shirts and baseball caps and whistles and armbands and a whole heap of other stuff.

'There's someone over there selling ice cream,' Fern said, shading her eyes against the sun. 'Who's for ice cream?'

'Me, if someone else goes and gets it,' Andy said.

Pippa agreed to go. We gave her our money and plenty of instructions about who wanted what flavour, and what flavour they wanted if their first choice wasn't available.

While we were waiting for Pippa to come back with our ice creams, I took out my tape recorder to give Cindy an update on our vacation.

Andy started off. 'Hi, Cindy, it's a totally brilliant day here at Camp Powhatan. The sun is shining and there isn't a cloud in the sky. But, hey! Wait! Coming over the trees!' He made his voice sound like he was in a big panic. 'It's a *twister*!'

'Andy, get real!' I said.

'It's coming closer!' Andy yelled into the machine. 'It's sucking up the cabins like they were made of matchwood. There goes the Chuckwagon. It's been smashed to pieces and it's raining hot dogs! It looks like we're all doomed! *He-e-e-elp*!'

Fern joined in, making *whooshing* and *sch-wooshing* noises and then following up with some crashing and crunching noises, like the twister was leaving a trail of destruction clear through the camp.

I grabbed the recorder from Andy. 'Cindy,' I said, trying to sound like someone in a disaster movie, 'Andy and Fern and Pippa have just been picked up by the twister. They're right up in the air. I can see Fern. She's waving. Oops! Andy's fallen out. He's going to hit the ground. Oh, no problem, he's landed on his head.'

'What's with Pippa?' Fern said.

'Beats me,' I said, 'she's up in the twister somewhere.'

'No,' Fern said. '*Really*! Look!'

I looked.

Pippa was racing up the slope towards us, and she had a look on her face that made me wonder if maybe a *real* twister was coming. And she didn't have any ice cream.

She came to a panting halt in front of us. Her face was bright red with running. She waved her arms about as she gasped for breath.

'LAINE!' she shrieked.

'You can call me Stacy,' I said. 'There's no one around to hear.'

'*No*!' Pippa hollered. 'Not *YOU! LAINE!*' She pointed towards the parking lot. 'The *real* Laine. Your cousin Laine. She's just pulled up in her car. She's *HERE*!'

'This is a joke, right?' I said.

Pippa stared at me. 'Do I look like I'm joking?'

'Trust me,' Fern said. 'She's not joking.'

'Oh, no!' I wailed. 'No, no, no, no!'

'Wait,' Andy said. 'It could be OK. I mean, how many people know what your sister Stacy is supposed to look like?'

'Only everyone who saw the picture that Amanda was showing around,' I said.

'Meaning how many?' Andy asked.

'Knowing Amanda,' I said, '*everyone*!'

'Hold it,' Pippa panted. 'This can still work so long as we get to Laine before anyone else does. We can explain everything to her and ask her to go along with it.'

'Yeah, you're right,' I said. 'Let's go!'

We raced down to the parking lot. Away over at the far side I could see a whole crowd of people. I couldn't see what they were crowding around, but I had a bad feeling that it was Laine.

I crashed into the back of the crowd and wormed my way through. Over the noise of people calling out, '*Can I have your autograph, Stacy*?' I could hear Laine.

'My name isn't *Stacy*,' she was yelling at the top of her voice. 'I don't know what you're all *talking* about. Is this some kind of initiation ceremony, or what?'

I managed to struggle through to where Laine was being pinned against her car.

'Stacy!' Laine exclaimed. 'Am I glad to see you! What kind of a mad house is this?'

I took a huge great deep breath.

'BACK OFF!' I yelled.

A small area cleared around Laine and me.

'Hi,' I said uneasily.

'Well, hi there, Stacy,' Laine said. She sounded kind of relieved that the crowd had quietened down. 'Do you want to fill me in? Why does everyone think I'm called Stacy?' She gave me a stern look that reminded me a little of Mom. 'And why do they all want my autograph?'

'Well, it's like this,' I said. 'It was Amanda. She—'

'Just wait one second!' It was a voice I recognized. A voice like a dentist's drill that I'd kind of hoped I wouldn't be hearing any more. I glanced round to see Andrea shoving her way out of the crowd.

She stood in front of Laine with her fists on her hips. 'Are you Stacy Allen, the TV star?' she said.

Laine laughed. 'Nope,' she said. 'I'm Laine Shelby Baxendale, the college student. And who are you?'

Andrea turned on me with a horribly triumphant look on her face.

'Ha!' she yelled, her finger almost poking right up my nose as she pointed at me. 'You and your sister and the whole darned bunch of you are nothing more than a load of total, utter and complete *liars*!'

Stacy to mothership, Stacy to mothership! Beam me up right NOW, please!

Chapter Sixteen

I was still trying to come up with some reasonable explanation for why cousin Laine wasn't really my TV-star sister, Stacy, when I heard someone pushing their way through the crowd.

'Laine!' Amanda gasped. 'I, I mean, *Stacy*.'

I looked at Amanda and shook my head. 'Too late,' I told her.

'Oh!'

Andrea sort of elbowed me aside and got right into Amanda's face. 'So you guys come from Beverly Hills, huh?' she shouted. She was making sure that everyone within a hundred *yards* could hear her. 'Like heck, you do! And your big sister is no TV star at all! Heck, she isn't even your real sister! Let me tell you, Amanda Allen, you didn't have me fooled for one single second!'

Now, I'd say that *most* people would either run for the hills or burst into tears after being yelled at like that in front of a couple of dozen people. Not Amanda!

'Get out of here!' Amanda yelled right back at Andrea. 'We had you fooled but good! It's *you* who didn't fool *us*! Did you really think we fell for all that boloney about the hotel in New York?'

'It just so happens that I *do* live where I said I live,' Andrea shouted. 'It's not *me* that's been lying my head off ever since I arrived here. It's *you*! You and those dumb, bird-brained freaks you hang out with.'

'Who are you calling a freak?' I yelled.

'Get lost, metalmouth,' Andrea snarled.

'You leave my sister alone,' Amanda snarled.

'Don't worry,' Andrea said. 'I wouldn't go near any of you with rubber gloves on! A person might get *contaminated* and end up as big a liar as you are!'

'I think that's *enough*!' Laine said. She stepped forward and got between Amanda and Andrea. 'I don't know what the problem is between you two, but bad-mouthing each other isn't going to solve it.'

For a moment it looked like Andrea and Amanda were going to pounce on each other like a pair of wildcats. But then Andrea shrugged.

'She's not worth the *effort*,' she said. 'I'm not prepared to lower myself to her level. I just think a big fat liar like her should be thrown out of the camp! That's what *I* think.'

Every eye was on Amanda, and everyone was waiting to hear what she'd say next.

But the thing that actually happened next took everyone completely by surprise. Well, *surprise* hardly covers it!

'Twinkle!' called a high, squeaky voice from somewhere at the back of the crowd. 'Twinkle, honey, it's Mommy.'

A small, round lady came trotting through the crowd. She was wearing an orange trouser suit and orange shoes. She even had orange-tinted hair. In fact, she was like the missing link between a human being and a real *orange*.

'Mom!' Andrea gasped.

'Twinkle!' squeaked the plump lady as she went up to Andrea and gave her a big hug. 'How are you, Twinkle, honey? Are you having a good time with all your new friends? Didn't I tell you you'd enjoy camp once you got here?'

We all just *stared* at the pair of them. Andrea's mom looked like a really nice lady, but she was no Olympic swimmer, that was for sure! And she didn't exactly look like the sort of person who'd just jetted back from a clothes show in Italy. She looked like a regular, everyday mom. A very *orange* mom!

And Andrea looked like she'd turned to stone. She didn't move. She didn't say a word. She just stood there as if she was waiting for the ground to open up and swallow her.

'I know you told me not to bother coming all the way down here,' Mrs Wolfson said, 'but I wanted to see just how much fun my Twinkle was having. Daddy couldn't get time off from the store, but I just had to drop everything and come visit my best girl.'

Amanda turned to Andrea's mom with a big smile.

'Hi, Mrs Wolfson,' she said. 'I'm really pleased to meet you. Andrea's told us so much about you.'

Mrs Wolfson smiled. 'Well, there's hardly anything to tell,' she said cheerfully. 'I guess Twinkle is *proud* of us, though. We run our own shoe store, you know. And it's the only shoe store in Littlestop.'

Littlestop? Was Littlestop a place in New York? Somehow I didn't think so. Littlestop sounded more like some small town out in the middle of nowhere.

Amanda looked at Andrea.

'You didn't tell us you had a nickname, Andrea,' she said with a smile so wide I thought it was going to meet around the back of her head. 'You've been holding out on us, *Twinkle*!'

'Mom,' Andrea said from between her teeth. 'I think I want to go now.'

'Go?' Mrs Wolfson said. 'What do you mean, darling? Go where?'

'Just *go*! OK?'

Andrea put an arm around her mother's shoulders and steered her out through the crowd. People backed off to let them pass.

We all watched in silence as Andrea and her mom walked over to an ordinary-looking orange car. They got in and as Andrea sat in the passenger seat I saw her curl up with her face in her hands.

'I guess there's no danger of anyone filling me in on what's been going on around here?' Laine asked.

'I want to say something to all of you,' Amanda announced loudly. She came over and put her arm around my shoulders. 'I just want to tell you that my sister Stacy and I don't come from Beverly Hills. And I want to apologize for making out that we did. I was just trying to get even with Andrea because of all her lies, and the whole thing got out of hand. I'm really sorry for not telling everyone the truth.'

There were plenty of annoyed-looking faces in the crowd. I guess people don't like to be made fools of. But at least Amanda was doing her best to straighten things out now.

'I hope you can forgive me,' Amanda continued. 'And I just want to say that Stacy here only went along with the stories to help me out, so you shouldn't blame her at all.'

There was a lot of murmuring and some really hard looks as the crowd broke up and we ended up on our own in the parking lot.

I didn't hear it leave, but when I looked around the Wolfsons' orange car had gone. I guessed that Andrea wasn't as brave as Amanda. I mean, Amanda may be one huge airhead, but at least she stood up in front of all those people and finally told them the truth. And that takes some nerve.

'You can start the explanation as soon as you feel up to it,' Laine said.

Amanda took a deep breath. 'Well,' she said. 'It's like this . . .'

* * *

Once we'd done all the explaining we had a pretty good day with cousin Laine, despite a few sour looks and sarcastic comments from some of the other people in the camp.

We didn't see Andrea or Mary-Beth again after Open Day. Like my mom would say, I guess they just weren't able to face the music. And it didn't take long for the story of what had happened in the parking lot to go around the whole camp.

I wouldn't say that Amanda and I and our friends were exactly camp favourites right away. I mean, it took a while for people to get over being told all those fibs. But most people understood Amanda's reasons for saying the things she did, because Andrea had been boasting her head off for a whole week before Amanda had even *arrived*. In fact, plenty of people thought Amanda was some kind of local hero for getting rid of the biggest boast-monster in the entire country.

So, how did the rest of our vacation go? Well, once Andrea and Mary-Beth had disappeared, things quickly got back to normal between me and my friends and Amanda and the Bimbos. Like, we remembered just how much we *hated the sight of each other!*

* * *

'Do you know what I like?' Fern whispered.

'No,' whispered Andy, 'what do you like?'

'I like *revenge*!'

The four of us were hiding behind some bushes. A few yards away the Bimbos were sitting at one of the wooden picnic tables, blabbing away and stuffing themselves with food.

I guess they were feeling pretty pleased with themselves because *someone* had put a very realistic-looking black rubber snake in my bed last night and I'd nearly screamed the place down before Fern had noticed it wasn't alive. And that *someone* was either Amanda or one of her dumb friends.

'Is everyone ready?' I asked.

'Check,' Pippa said.

'Ready,' Fern said.

'Let's go,' Andy said.

How did I *know* it was one of them? Well, if a person sneaks into the showers while four well-known Bimbos are in there, and if that person turns the hot water off so that the Bimbos get a freezing cold shower, then that person kind of expects some retaliation. The rubber snake was their revenge.

'OK,' I said. 'Mark your target. Splat 'em good and then get out of there!'

Each of us held a paper plate piled high with cream from a spray can of whipped cream that we'd bought in the camp store.

'Go!'

We jumped out from behind the bushes and ran at the Bimbos, yelling and whooping.

Fifteen seconds later the whole area looked like an explosion in a cream factory and we were running like crazy with four cream-splattered Bimbos hot on our heels.

'Just think,' Fern panted as we tried to outrun the crazy-homicidal-screaming-and-hollering Bimbos. 'If Camp Yellowhammer hadn't been flooded, we'd have missed all this fun!'

'Yeah,' Andy gasped as Cheryl's fingers just missed grabbing hold of the back of his collar. 'And I wouldn't have missed this for the *world*!'

I couldn't help laughing. Do you know something? I think he was *right*!